P9-DIJ-559

Silas and Ben-Godik

Books by Cecil Bødker
(available in English translation)

SILAS AND THE BLACK MARE
SILAS AND BEN-GODIK
SILAS AND THE RUNAWAY COACH
THE LEOPARD

Silas and *Ben-Godik*

Cecil Bødker

Translated from the Danish by
Sheila La Farge

A Merloyd Lawrence Book
DELACORTE PRESS/SEYMOUR LAWRENCE

A MERLOYD LAWRENCE BOOK
Published by
Delacorte Press/Seymour Lawrence
1 Dag Hammarskjold Plaza
New York, N.Y. 10017

Originally published in Danish by Branner og Korch,
Copenhagen, Denmark under the title *Silas og Ben-Godik.*
Copyright © 1969 by Branner og Korch

English translation copyright © 1978 by Dell Publishing Co., Inc.

Manufactured in the United States of America

First U.S.A. printing

Designed by Laura Bernay

Library of Congress Cataloging in Publication Data

Bødker, Cecil.
Silas and Ben-Godik.

Translation of Silas og Ben-Godik.
"A Merloyd Lawrence book."
SUMMARY: Silas and his friend Ben-Godik
spend a year traveling by horseback and encounter-
ing many strange individuals and harrowing ad-
ventures.
          I.   Title.
PZ7.B635717Sg   [Fic]   78-50459
          ISBN 0-440-07923-3
          ISBN 0-440-07924-1 lib. bdg.

CONTENTS

Silas and Ben-Godik

ONE

The town by the sea

ALL THE REST of the summer Silas and Ben-Godik traveled around the country riding their horses from town to town, from place to place, up over high ridges covered with heather, down long, grassy valleys with houses scattered on the slopes, into forests and out across broad, desolate stretches. Always in almost the same direction as the river, always farther and farther away from Ben-Godik's village.

It was a big country.

Though they rode in the same direction as the river, they did not follow it. The roads zigzagged between the inhabited places farther inland; only occasionally would they come upon the riverbank, where they could see the fast-flowing water. It took a long time to cross these vast areas.

1

But Silas was happy. Never before had he enjoyed himself so much. Throughout his childhood he had accompanied his mother and Philip the sword-swallower, so he was used to a wandering life; they had never lived for very many days at a time in any one place, therefore he could not see anything strange about the life he was leading now with Ben-Godik. On the contrary: surely nothing could be better than roaming around on your own horse with no one telling you what to do. Silas rejoiced at his good fortune. Not only had he won the horse, but he had got her back when the villagers took her away from him—and besides, now he had Ben-Godik with him. That was almost the best.

When they came to a group of houses where they wanted to stay the night, Silas would play his flute and perform in an open place, just as he had done when traveling with Philip. That way he earned money for food and a place to sleep. It was so simple and so logical that he could see no reason to do anything else. People very seldom saw real performers and Silas noticed with quiet joy that he could make an entire village turn out to see his stunts.

It was different for Ben-Godik; he had never been very far from his village and had never ridden long distances for any length of time and, besides, he was of a different disposition than his companion. Ben-Godik could not stop worrying.

Naturally, in the beginning he had found the life they were leading unique and marvelous not only because he did not have to look after the village cattle but because with Silas he could ride exactly where he felt like going. But gradually, as the days and weeks passed and as autumn came near without Silas appearing to have even thought of turning back to the village, Ben-Godik was seized by homesickness. At the same time he was attacked by a guilty conscience because he had ridden off without knowing how things had worked out for his mother and his younger brothers and sisters. He had assumed all along that Aaron the otter hunter would look after them—but what if he hadn't? What if Bartolin had done him some harm? Those two were certainly not friends—and his mother had not cared for Bartolin.

She might also be worried about him, Ben-Godik. He had left the village so suddenly that there had been no time for explanations. The villagers had been so infuriated when Silas had tricked them out of the horse that it was essential to get away fast.

All summer long Ben-Godik kept his thoughts to himself, but the further into autumn they progressed, the more these thoughts tormented him, until finally he had to discuss them with Silas. Besides, his bad foot hurt. The cold and windy weather combined with their poor clothing made his foot ache, and even though perhaps they couldn't return to the village, they might at least move into a house.

Silas thought they certainly could do that. They could take lodging somewhere, he said, but they had to be in a real town, a big town where they could find ways to make ends meet all winter. He knew where they could find such a town: all they had to do was go on to where the river opened out into the ocean; it wasn't very far.

Ben-Godik nodded in silence and wrapped a big wad of straw around his foot. Since he wasn't going to get home, a couple of miles more or less didn't make much difference. Except for the fact that he was freezing. But they both were; their clothes were not suitable for winter weather, and to ward off the worst cold, they stuffed straw both up into their shirts and down into their trousers until they looked like scarecrows.

Silas said that they had to have new clothes when they got to the town.

Ben-Godik nodded silently, said nothing to contradict him—though he knew how expensive clothes were.

But Silas was someone who knew how to go about things. To be sure, he had never been to this town before, but he had traveled through other big ones with Philip, and the first, most important thing was to make people notice you.

"You can't rent lodgings if you don't have money," he said.

So when they came to the outskirts of the town, Silas took out his flute and, standing on the back of the black mare, proceeded down the streets playing music until he reached the town square. Happy and cheerful, he let himself be carried along on his beautiful horse, who automatically switched to an easy, graceful dancing gait when she heard the flute.

Ben-Godik stayed modestly right behind him. Neither he nor his shaggy, short-legged horse had any talent for that sort of performance. Instead, he looked around gaping, for he had never been in a town the likes of this before. It was frighteningly large and teeming full of people compared to places he knew. For fear of losing his way in the innumerable streets, he stayed as close behind the black mare as he dared, acutely aware of what a strange impression both he and Silas made in their clothes stuffed with straw, bristling out here and there. But such things did not bother Silas. On the contrary: the worse they looked, the better they could catch people's attention and rouse their curiosity.

But even though the shaggy horse had proved to be totally impervious to training, the music was truly not without an effect on him. Quite simply, Shags loved the flute more than anything in the world, and there was nothing he would not do to get hold of it. Ben-Godik was obliged to keep a firm grip on the reins all the time to prevent him from dashing over to Silas, open-mouthed in his eagerness to munch the shiny, dark wooden object.

This remarkable creature didn't resemble any other horse they had ever met. He had his own very personal —not always admirable—way of attracting attention. In addition to his weakness for finely polished woodwork, he had developed a powerful inclination toward open doors and windows. More than once Ben-Godik had to back him out of people's houses, while the agitated family swung their household utensils threateningly at both him and the horse.

Occasionally, while passing by, Shags would also manage to poke his long, impudent head into a window facing the road. At best, some otherwise peaceable woman would become terrified and scream to high heaven; at worst the horse would grab the vegetables for her soup or a loaf of bread cooling from the oven. This old nag always knew just how to get them into trouble but still they wouldn't have exchanged him for all the world.

Ben-Godik gripped the reins desperately hard while Silas headed the black mare into the square. Here they had to be careful not to get into trouble, for it was here that they were going to stay and in such a big town there was bound to be both a bailiff and guards close at hand.

When people began to crowd around, Silas pulled the straw out from under his clothes and threw it down in a heap on the cobbles so that he could move more freely. A bitterly cold wind was blowing off the ocean, a wind full of strange smells which made both Ben-Godik and Shags stretch their necks and sniff. It smelled of salt water and washed-up seaweed and rotting fish. Shags wanted to head straight for the ocean; the smells attracted him, but Ben-Godik kept him firmly at the outer edge of the spectators. He didn't dare lose sight of Silas.

In the center of the circle Silas went through his performance. Ben-Godik tried to judge the effect. People seemed to enjoy it; in any case they applauded eagerly and several times Silas was able to collect coins from the rough, uneven cobblestones. Otherwise Ben-Godik could not see much of what was happening in the center, but suddenly he caught sight of a tall, rawboned woman craning her neck to see over the others, all the while clutching a little boy. Her bony yellow fingers were closed around one of his upper arms and this obviously hurt him. It was also obvious that the boy didn't dare protest. He was no bigger than Ben-Godik's little brother at home, and he dangled from the end of the woman's arm like a rag doll.

Ben-Godik stared at her. Why didn't she let the boy stand on his own—or why didn't she lift him up so that he could see something too? He was much shorter than anyone around him.

Old witch, thought Ben-Godik, glowering at her fiercely, and the more he stared the more extraordinary she seemed. On her head she wore a large, broad-brimmed man's hat with a whole lot of gray wisps of hair sticking out from under the brim, hair which had certainly not been combed either today or yesterday. Her long, thin face could just as well have belonged to a man, Ben-Godik felt, and her heavy, floppy skirts reached down to the tops of a pair of worn-out soldier's boots, while on the upper part of her body she wore something most like a coachman's cape. A weird figure.

The boy looked as if he were no more than seven or eight years old, a little thing, thin-legged, with huge, terrified eyes and cheeks that were blue from the cold. The woman who had hold of his arm towered above him.

Ben-Godik stared so long and intently at this remarkable pair that she finally noticed. With an angry toss of her head she turned her eagle-beak of a nose around, planting her black eyes on him like a couple of cannon-balls. She was obviously not to be trifled with.

"What are you staring at?" she asked.

"He can't see anything," replied Ben-Godik, pointing to the boy. "He's welcome to sit up here with me."

Ben-Godik rode over near her.

"He doesn't need to," she answered in a curt, un-friendly way.

Shags lowered his head and sniffed her and com-

7

pletely forgot that he had wanted to be down by the docks.

"But he can't see anything," Ben-Godik tried again. He felt very sorry for the youngster who dangled as though she were in the process of squeezing the life out of him.

"Is that any of your business?" she asked.

Shags blew rapturously right down into her boot and sank exploring teeth into the calf of her leg.

"Stop that, you devil!" shouted the crone, pounding one clenched fist against the horse's hard skull.

He squinted at her beatifically through wisps of his forelock but she spun around on her worn-down soldier's heels, seething with rage, and marched off dragging the boy, who almost had to walk sideways.

Ben-Godik was still sitting on Shags watching them go when Silas came over and asked whether he was woolgathering. Ben-Godik came to with a start and Silas jingled the coins in his pocket triumphantly. It had been a good day; he had even got the address of an old deaf lady who was said both to rent rooms and also have an outbuilding in the yard behind her house.

"On Fisherman Street," Silas informed him.

Neither of them knew where Fisherman Street was to be found, but it was bound to be near the harbor.

Suddenly Ben-Godik grabbed Silas by the arm. "Look over there!"

Silas looked around startled.

"What should I look at?"

"Those two."

"The knife-grinder woman?"

"And the boy," said Ben-Godik, all agitated. "Can't you see that she has hitched him to her cart?"

Silas grinned.

"Calm down, loads of children have their work cut out for them at that age. Didn't you?"

"Yes, but that woman—" Ben-Godik went on looking at the boy in the harness in front of the knife-grinder's heavy, green cart with the grindstone. There was something about the boy's despondency that made it all look wrong.

"She's probably his grandmother," said Silas. "She has a right to do that."

"What's your name?" asked Ben-Godik as they rode by.

The boy started and glanced nervously back at the knife-grinder in the broad-brimmed hat.

"I'm Jonah and she's my grandmother," he reeled off.

"There, you see," said Silas.

The bony face under the big hat smiled threateningly.

Ben-Godik kept his thoughts to himself and when, shortly after, they reached the house on Fisherman Street and had to negotiate with the deaf lady, he forgot about it. For it became apparent that the deaf lady was deafer than they had thought; she could only understand what they were saying when they agreed to her terms. She pointed to the horses excitedly.

"Yes, indeed, the horses need a place to sleep, too," maintained Silas.

The woman clutched her head in dismay and pointed up the narrow loft stairs. Did they intend to keep the horses up there with them? she wanted to know.

Silas pointed to a ramshackle building over in her backyard. It appeared to be a partially ruined stable that had not been used for a long time; it looked terrible. The deaf lady stared at him uncomprehendingly. Then, resolutely, Silas dug a jingling handful out of his pocket and shook that in her face. The woman grabbed his wrist to see, then she nodded and pawed the coins out of his hand. They could start settling in right away, she said, flip-flopping back across the yard in her home-sewn carpet slippers.

"They said it was lodgings," muttered Ben-Godik thoughtfully when, a little later, they could see the deaf lady standing counting the coins inside by her kitchen table.

"Don't be a stickler about that kind of thing," said Silas, glancing down the rotten fence separating the deaf lady's backyard from the neighboring yards. "We have a roof over our heads now and that's the most important thing."

"Yes, but an empty loft—for so much money?"

"That's the way it is in all real towns," Silas pointed out, shrugging. He didn't understand why Ben-Godik became dejected over so little.

"Even straw for bedding costs money here," Ben-Godik went on. "Don't you think we should have found a place in a country village instead?"

"Well, it's also much easier to earn a living here than out in the country," Silas supposed. "People have more money on them."

Ben-Godik went right on thinking that the town was strange; there were far too many people and he didn't know a single one of them. And up in the loft where they were to stay it was totally bare and not at all cozy.

"If we fetch our own straw from outside of town, we'll get it cheaply," said Silas. "It's a matter of always having money."

Ben-Godik sighed. Yes, money. He was never the one who earned what they needed and that pained him a little. At home the whole family had been dependent on what he earned; now it was almost of no consequence. Sometimes he felt strangely useless.

They took a quick look in at the rotten stable and decided to go get straw immediately, both for themselves and for the horses, and to get as much as possible, for the weather was fairly cold and they had no bedding of any kind.

Neither Silas nor Ben-Godik had seen the ocean before, so first, out of pure curiosity, they rode out along the beach while they breathed in the strong salt air with obvious pleasure. Even the horses looked as if they enjoyed it, and they let them trot along on the hard sand right down by the water's edge. A beach like this one was a marvelous sandy place unlike anywhere they had ever been, all strewn about with things that had drifted ashore. In one place there was an old, battered fishing boat, which they looked at for a long time, but unfortunately it appeared beyond repair, and somewhere else, part of a coach. Scattered over the entire beach were branches and wooden posts and broken barrels and every conceivable scrap of wood mixed with whatever else had washed up from the ocean floor. When they

11

came upon the severed stump of a wooden beam, Ben-Godik dismounted and picked it up.

"Leave it!" Silas shouted to him. "We can't have a fire in the loft anyway; there's no stove—or we'd have plenty of firewood for several years."

He pointed to the tidemark of washed-up things, an unbroken border extending down along the shoreline as far as the eye could see.

Ben-Godik followed the direction of his pointing finger and nodded silently. Something began to move inside him. And as if Silas had read his thoughts, he too dismounted and picked up a piece of wood. It was only a small block but nice, solid wood and he handed it to Ben-Godik.

"I need a bowl," he said. "Could you carve me one?"

Ben-Godik raised his head with a start and all the bowls and dishes that he had carved over the years came loose in his heart. They were one of the reasons why he longed for home. There had been no time for that kind of work since he had left his village, and his hands badly needed to feel something take shape again, obedient to their will. Without hesitating he took the wood that Silas offered him.

"But it is not to be just an ordinary bowl," said Silas. "It has to have a broad, flat piece sticking out on one side."

"A handle?" asked Ben-Godik.

"No—or at least not an ordinary handle. It has to be horizontal."

"I've never seen a bowl like that," protested Ben-Godik in surprise.

12

"The black mare is the one who will use it."

"To drink from?"

"To collect money in," laughed Silas. "It has to be good and deep. No one has ever seen a horse collect its own pay before—and so many people always stand and stare and then just walk away."

Now Ben-Godik laughed too.

"You certainly do always come up with something," he said. Inside he felt deep joy at the prospect of using his knife again for something other than cutting bread. He tied the block of wood securely to Shags' harness and hurried after Silas, who had set off at a gallop in the direction of a farmhouse hidden behind a grove of trees a short distance inland.

When Ben-Godik eventually reached the house, Silas was already busy bargaining with the farmer over a big pile of straw bundles for which there was no storage space in the barn. Silas and the farmer were standing in the middle of the farmyard, and in the doorway leading to the kitchen stood the farmer's plump wife with a couple of little children staring timidly at the strangers. Two somewhat bigger children and an old geezer with cow manure way up his trouser legs quietly appeared out the barn door but no one dared approach Silas and the farmer. From a distance, Ben-Godik could hear what Silas was working on.

Even before they had agreed on a price for the straw, he was busy enlarging on his own and his horse's excellence and on everything they could do together.

The farmer looked incredulous and glanced over at his own horses standing idly in the field.

"I wonder whether you're not lying a little."

Raising his fingers, Silas swore indignantly. "What do you bet?"

The farmer hesitated. Betting was a dangerous thing, that he knew—you could lose.

"A portion of that soup which smells so good?" asked Silas.

The farmer smiled with relief, that was not much. "Certainly," he said.

"One for him too?"

Silas pointed over to Ben-Godik, who was carefully keeping Shags just outside the farmyard.

"Yes, yes!" the farmer exclaimed impatiently, for they did have plenty of soup. "Just begin!"

Silas took out his flute. "No celebration without music," he stated, and even that struck the farmer and his family as marvelous and rare. They were not used to music, certainly not to such music as Silas drew out of his instrument. They stood as if glued to the houses, wide-eyed and gaping, taking it all in while absolutely motionless, as if they expected the flute player to stop if they moved.

For these were the very sounds of life's great occasions, associated in their minds with solemnity and festivity. Yet here they were in their very own farmyard on a very ordinary day dressed in their work clothes listening to it. Such a thing could only seem alarming—yes, even almost blasphemous to the good family's peace of mind, for there was no dead person to be buried and honored with a meal and there was no wedding being performed; they could not even produce a child to be baptized. And yet they let themselves be waited on with flute-playing.

14

Silas called the mare.

Almost without stopping the music, he mounted her and bade her do what no farm horse would ever think of, bade her dance and curtsey and rear up, while the farmer's family kept back against the walls in a daze, overcome by the extraordinary sight.

"And that is just a choice selection of what the mare can do, just a sample," said Silas, as the farmer had to come over and stroke the matchless animal and marvel over her, as different as could be from his old nags.

And then finally they could go along in and eat. To be sure, all they could offer them was very ordinary soup of the day with coarse bread, the farmer explained apologetically.

Silas and Ben-Godik thanked him. As they had not eaten in rather a long time, they were famished, and Silas performed a series of cartwheels clear across the yard from sheer enthusiasm. The soup of the day in the country was simple, substantial fare, that he knew well, with a lot in it.

After the meal, he fished out his coins and wanted to pay for the straw but there was no question of his doing so. The farmer waved it aside with his hands, that small pile of straw amounted to nothing; he was the one who should be thankful for all the music and everything else there had been to see. He murmured something to one of the bigger boys, and the fellow dashed out the door with alarming speed and went clear around the house out of sight. Ben-Godik and Silas glanced at each other.

But they could have spared themselves their concern. The boy came rushing back with a squawking, flapping young cockerel fresh from the dungheap, with straw and manure dangling between its claws; he handed it to the farmer, who without a word wrung the creature's neck and gave it right to Silas.

"Here," he said, "take this too—and come back another time. . . . Straw we have plenty of."

After that he helped them load straw bundles onto the horses and tie them fast one on top of the other until finally the horses looked like wandering haystacks with legs. Then, walking alongside, Silas and Ben-Godik gradually made their way back to town, where they immediately began to arrange the best corner of the deplorable stable into winter quarters for the horses.

"Now that was a fine farmer, wasn't he?" said Ben-Godik thoughtfully. "Couldn't we have lived with him?"

"You shouldn't kill the goose that lays the golden eggs," replied Silas. "It's better to have him in reserve. There are not many like him."

Ben-Godik did not completely understand what he meant but he lifted a straw bundle onto his back and limped over toward the loft stairs. After that he took another over. Up in the loft he spread out the straw down at one end where there was a small gable window and where the roof looked as if it was moderately tight. It might do for winter quarters, he thought, though he would have preferred a little more light. He sat down in the pile of straw and looked carefully at the piece of wood they had found on the beach. To collect money in, he thought. Silas was always the one who collected the money, Silas and the horse. If only he had some of all the bowls and dishes that he had stashed in his cave by the river at home, he could have sold them—and earned some money himself.

The thought took fire in him.

True enough, he couldn't get hold of the dishes—but he could carve new ones. He had his knife and his hands and he knew how to use both.

His decision was a silent one. He didn't say anything to Silas, but he knew that they would spend a lot of money quickly—they needed blankets and clothes and food for themselves and the animals.

Without waiting any longer he groped in his pocket, found his pocketknife and began to whittle the wood, which was still slightly damp; once again he felt that wonderful sensation of something yielding to his will. The wood shavings curled out and fell off, leaving a useful object in his hands.

The very next day he decided to ride down to the beach again. If he had found one piece of wood that would do, surely he could find others, and even if it wasn't the very finest, he would take trouble over the bowl for Silas. Although almost no light came in through that little window, he was still completely absorbed in his work when the other boy finally came upstairs.

TWO

What the deaf lady hid under her firewood

ALL WINTER SILAS and Ben-Godik lived in the old deaf lady's cold loft, which proved to be even less weatherproof and even colder than they had thought. Of course they realized that they could not expect to live in real luxury, but all the same, when the cold weather set in for good, it was almost too much. It was as if the cold here by the sea was of a different and more penetrating kind than further inland.

"It's all this fog," lamented Ben-Godik, rubbing his foot.

"And then it's always blowing," agreed Silas.

For not only did it rain in through the roof above them, but, to make matters worse, the raw ocean wind whistled in all around below, and if it snowed, innumerable long, thin drifts blew in across the partially rotten plank floor that separated the loft from the rooms below. As quickly as possible the boys had to scrape up the wet white piles and throw them out the little gable window before they melted.

For a while they smirked at the deaf lady in the hopes of being allowed to move downstairs in the worst weather. But that was really out of the question.

In the first place, the house itself was not particularly large. Facing the street the deaf lady had only her parlor, which she never once had the heart to use herself; facing the yard was the kitchen and a tiny back room crammed full to the door with firewood for the stove.

And in the second place, she completely failed to grasp what they were talking about whenever they even began to approach the subject. It was totally impossible for her to comprehend what they wanted even though she appeared to try her very best.

So they stopped. Quite simply, they saw for themselves how impossible their longing was, because the kitchen was the only warm place in the house and that was where she lived. There she ate her meals at the white wood table which had been scoured and scoured so long that the grain of the wood stood out like a ribbed pattern; there she spent her days and there she slept at night. Along the wall facing the parlor a kind of alcove had been built, a sleeping cupboard with a curtain around it. And in the little room off the kitchen she stored all her firewood. There was nothing to be done; they just had to stay where they were even though their teeth were chattering.

But Silas would not have been Silas and Ben-Godik

would not have been Ben-Godik if they had let themselves freeze to death just like that next to each other in a stranger's loft. The miserable circumstances roused their resourcefulness and little by little they began to try to improve on them. First they noticed that the drifts of snow melted fastest over the kitchen where the stove was, meaning that it had to be warmer there, so that was where they moved their sleeping place. At least a little warmth came up from downstairs even though the draft that whistled through the otherwise empty loft space tormented them. They lacked any kind of partitioned sleeping place.

This was solved one day when Silas came home with a couple of worn-out horse blankets which he had bought for not much money. They were all shiny with grease from the horses and so stiff that they could hardly be rolled up, but that didn't bother the boys. They thought the blankets could make their sleeping quarters snug and, using a system of punched holes and splints of wood, they attached the blankets to each other and rigged them up under the roof like a kind of tent over the straw pile. The space under the tent was far from roomy, they had to crawl in on all fours, but by stretching the blankets well out to the sides and weighing down the edges with stones and, not least, by scraping together the leftover straw and putting it as far up the sides as possible, they increased the temperature inside the tent quite noticeably.

But the most fantastic coup was achieved by Ben-Godik when, with the help of his pocketknife, he loosened one of the less good boards of the loft floor over the kitchen. It turned out that the board could easily be loosened at one end and, by wedging the stick in the crack, they could keep it open and get some of the stale air from the deaf lady's kitchen to fill the tent. And though certainly not all the air that came up through the crack smelled good, the two boys luxuriated in the heat from the deaf lady's stove without her having the slightest suspicion that they were benefiting from it. Every evening when darkness began to settle in the corners, they would stealthily slip the stick in place, and every morning at daybreak they removed it again—and every single night they slept well without freezing.

"That is what is called adapting oneself to circumstances," said Silas.

In the mornings, weather permitting, he trained the black mare in the deaf lady's small backyard. He could see her sitting inside watching through the window and Silas was happy to grant her what little entertainment she could derive from watching him. Such an old, lonely woman wouldn't have very much to fill her life.

Meanwhile Ben-Godik sat in the stable where he had arranged a corner for himself next to the horses. There they also had had to use their inventiveness to block out the cold, for the entire roof had collapsed on one end of the old building and the wind and weather stormed right in. But by using the tumbled-down material, they built a partition between the good and bad parts of the stable, so that now at least the end where the horses were was weatherproof. And the big, hot animals could warm the air themselves with their own bodies. It was a pleasure to come in there in the morning

21

after both of them had been standing glowing with heat all night and besides, it was not as dark down there as up in the loft.

In the beginning, Silas performed in different places around town almost every afternoon and often he earned quite a lot from his performances, especially when he had taught the mare to carry Ben-Godik's wooden bowl around among the spectators. That, after all, was something they had never seen before and they simply could not resist it.

But eventually as time passed and the cold weather came, people lost interest in watching his stunts, partly of course because they had seen him before and knew what he could do and partly because it was too cold to stand still for so long in the wind. And windy it certainly was, all the time.

But just as the interest in Silas died down, the demand for Ben-Godik's bowls and dishes began to grow, and more and more the earning of the money they needed came to depend on his skillful handiwork.

And Ben-Godik needed this. He simply could not stop; ever since he had set out from home he had been merely someone who trailed along, but now suddenly he mattered and was responsible for something. Now he was the one who saw to it that they did not starve. And the ladies in the town contemplated his woodwork with favorable and expert eyes; they knew what was good, knew how to evaluate such things, and when they paid they felt that they were really getting something for their money.

Ben-Godik would come home happy and in fine fettle

to show a dark, withdrawn Silas what he had in his pockets. But he also took great pains with what he made. Long before, he had got himself a gouge and other tools from the local blacksmith, which simplified his work and meant that he could make the bowls much more even inside, and in addition he got to know how to choose the wood so that the darker grain would end up making a pattern in the bottom of the bowl—or he might take it into his head to give the utensils a little carved outer rim. All of this increased the women's desire to buy.

When Silas finally realized that performing with the horse on the streets at this season would not work, he contented himself with keeping the mare in form with a short training session every morning, after which he took over half of Ben-Godik's work, namely the selling. It was no secret to either of them that Silas could sell more, and more quickly, thanks to his aptitude for talking with people. No one knew the right words in the right places as he did, and since in addition he was better at walking than the limping Ben-Godik, they found this division of labor made sense.

And thus a long time passed.

Ben-Godik whittled for all he was worth and Silas offered his wares for sale and gradually they got to know the town from the back side as well—quite literally from the side that it turned in toward the yards, where life was lived most of the time. A traveling merchant would not go to the front door if he had any real hope of selling anything, and so Silas would walk in through the gates, around behind the houses, and into the kitchens where he could make a display of what he had brought along, and where the ladies could pick and choose in peace so that they would get exactly what they needed.

And soon there began to be a little money left over after they had paid the deaf lady for their lodgings. Only small change, needless to say, but still enough for them to find it wise to wrap it in a piece of horse blanket in the deaf lady's loft. It was always good to have something in reserve for the day when they might lose this comparatively secure life.

One dark evening long after they had crawled into their sleeping tent, and when the deaf lady down below had also gone to bed, there was a cautious tapping knock on the kitchen windowpane. The boys up in the loft were wide awake at once and listened breathlessly through the crack in the floor. What was happening now?

The faint tapping sounded again and neither Ben-Godik nor Silas was in doubt that someone really was knocking; it was not an accidental noise.

But who would want to see the deaf lady at this time of night? If it was people who knew her, surely they would never think that they could wake her with such timid mouse noises since she couldn't hear anything— but if they were strangers, why didn't they go to the door?

The tapping sounded again. And it occurred to Silas to go down and tell them that they might as well save their energy, whoever they were, but at that very moment the deaf lady got out of bed down in the kitchen and felt around the floor with her feet for the worn-out slippers that she always shuffled about in.

Silas laid a cautioning hand on Ben-Godik's arm. The tapping on the windowpane was sharp, almost scolding; the deaf lady suppressed an oath and made do with the one carpet slipper that she had fumbled for and found in the dark. With this on one foot and nothing on the other she hurried out to her back door and opened it. Silas grabbed Ben-Godik's arm excitedly. She had heard.

Down below in the dark a man's voice cursed the woman's tardiness in an offended tone and demanded some light.

"Hush." The deaf lady whispered for him to be silent.

"What the devil is going on?" asked the man, lowering his voice a little. "Do you have someone in the house again?"

"Up in the loft."

The deaf lady raked a glowing coal out of the stove and lit a taper and the crack under the loose plank let a pale gleam of light up into the tent between Silas and Ben-Godik.

"But didn't I tell you that we don't want that," the man whispered. "It's much too dangerous—"

"Not as long as you keep your mouth shut," the deaf lady groused back in an unfriendly way. "These two can't do any harm anyway; they're just a couple of boys."

"Where in the loft?" the man wanted to know.

"Way over by the gable, or that's where they put the straw when they came."

She was obviously not the sort that bothers to run up and down stairs, Silas could tell, or at least she hadn't been up there since they had moved over above the kitchen.

"Hang something over the window," ordered the man.

"That would look suspicious," the deaf lady protested, "and who would be standing out in this cold?"

"Hang something up when I tell you to," said the man sternly. And the boys up in the loft could hear the old woman irritatedly pulling a blanket off her bed.

"Hurry it up a little," the man went on impatiently. "We can't take all night—you take so damn long to wake up. The watchman went inside just now, and they're waiting down with the boat. . . . We have to be off before he comes back."

"Yes, yes, yes. . . ."

The conversation was carried on in an annoyed half-whisper and every single word could be heard quite clearly by the boys lying rigid with excitement, listening with their whole bodies. Ordinarily the deaf lady could only take in what they shouted at the top of their lungs. Now they hardly even dared breathe for fear she would hear.

"How many will go this time?" asked the woman.

"Four," replied the man curtly. And the deaf lady began to move pieces of firewood into the kitchen.

If Silas had dared turn over in the straw he might have been able to see what was happening down below, but he didn't dare. That man sounded malevolent.

"It's certainly taking time," he grumbled. "You really stashed it way back there, damn you."

"Do you want it lying out in plain sight?" snapped the woman. "Boys like that have eyes in their heads, after all!"

26

"Then why do you have them here? Get rid of them, I told you."

"They're what I live on," came the dry, unequivocal words from the deaf lady as she put something heavy down on the kitchen floor with a groan.

"Live on?" the man fumed scornfully.

"Otherwise there could be trouble for you and yours if I were less prudent," said the woman, bringing more heavy things into the room.

Then she asked, "Four?"

"We'll fetch the rest next time," said the man.

"Have you someone to help you?" she asked.

"He's out by the gate. We can take two each."

The old woman began stacking her firewood back in her little room again, and the man shouted an order out the door to his helper. Shortly after the boys heard someone move away from the house with almost soundless steps.

But still Silas did not dare move, though they would have liked to creep over to the little gable window and try to see what the man was taking away with him. Only when the deaf lady had cleared and swept, closed the back room, and gone to bed herself and they could hear her distinct snores, did they dare whisper about what had happened.

"What do you think it was?" asked Ben-Godik.

"It sounded like sacks, I think."

"Of what?"

"I don't know. They are going to be sailed across— across where?"

"The river?" suggested Ben-Godik. "Or the ocean?"

27

"What do you think it was?"

"She has more of it down there," said Ben-Godik thoughtfully.

"Someday when she is not there—" Silas began.

"But she always is. She almost never goes out."

"Then we'll have to make her," whispered Silas.

"How?"

They went on whispering for a long time without making head or tail of it. All they knew for certain was that the deaf lady was definitely not deaf, and that she had something down there which was dangerous to have.

The following evenings they lay waiting for the man to return for the rest of it as he said he would, but nothing happened. And the deaf lady heard just as badly as she ever had.

As if coincidentally, Silas began to frequent the harbor district with his dishes and bowls. He boarded the ships, but the sailors just smiled at him and sent him back to shore. Nowhere did Silas catch a glimpse of anything unusual, or of people acting secretively.

Then he tried in a harborside tavern to see if they might need bowls and dishes, while asking what was across the ocean.

"A country," he was told.

"Could I go there?" he asked further.

"Why do you want to, since you wouldn't be able to understand what they say over there?"

"Why not?" asked Silas, pretending to be stupid.

"They talk differently."

"I've often heard people who talk differently, but I can still understand them."

"Yes, but over there they have a completely different language. Try talking to that man there," said the waiter, pointing to a sailor who had just stepped in.

Silas took out a bundle of spoons from among the dishes and asked the stranger politely whether he wanted to buy one.

The sailor waved his hands and came out with a whole lot of curious sounds, while everyone present burst into laughter over that fine language.

Silas put a questioning expression on his face and held the spoons toward the man in an offering way and made him realize that he could buy one.

The foreigner dug a coin out of his pocket and gave it to Silas, chose a spoon and pushed the boy aside.

Silas rejoiced soundlessly. It was a foreign coin, just as he had hoped. He closed his fist tight around it and rushed off with his load. This was what he needed. And without trying to sell any more that day, he hurried home and ran headlong, out of breath, into the deaf lady in her kitchen.

She looked sharply and questioningly at him.

Silas said that he had a message for her.

"What's that you say?" Putting her hand behind her ear, she tried to gather what he wanted of her.

Silas shouted as loudly as he could that a man wished to talk with her.

The deaf lady shook her head confusedly but her eyes developed a watchful glint.

"What is it?"

Silas repeated the message.

"What kind of man?"

"I didn't know him."

"What did you say?"

"I didn't know him!" screamed Silas.

"Where was he?"

"Down by the harbor."

"You're trying to put something over on me," argued the deaf lady, staring at him mistrustfully.

Silas shrugged as if he didn't care. Then he pretended to suddenly remember the coin and he held it out to her as proof.

The deaf lady stared at him penetratingly, unmistakably trying to weigh the pros and cons. Was what he said true or did he only want to fool her? She took the coin and studied it at length and was none the wiser. Then suddenly it looked as if she came to a conclusion, for she let her face light up with a happy smile.

"It must be my son; he must have come back. It can't be anyone else."

Silas completely lost his nerve—she sounded so convincing—but then he met her gaze, which was still full of crafty suspicion.

"Where did you see him?" she wanted to know.

Silas suddenly thought of a shed for fishing tackle that he had seen; it might be a suitable place. Half-shouting, he described it.

"Where?"

Silas repeated as loudly as he could. They both knew that she didn't have a son. The deaf lady began feverishly to root out her shawl and a woolen head covering that almost concealed her whole face. She appeared convincingly deaf while she fumbled around not knowing how best to hurriedly get him to believe in the son who had appeared so suddenly.

She hesitated for a moment by the door as if considering whether to lock it, then she abandoned the idea and Silas strolled in his most casual manner across the yard without so much as turning.

No sooner was she out the gate than Silas ran the last part of the way over to Ben-Godik in the stable and tossed the wooden utensils down on the floor noisily.

"Hurry up!" he shouted.

"With what?" Ben-Godik didn't move.

"Now she's gone."

"Where?"

"I'll tell you later, come on."

Ben-Godik dropped what he was working on and together the two ran back to the kitchen after first having made sure that the deaf lady really had gone down the street. Quickly they started searching through the firewood in the back room. Silas handed the logs out to Ben-Godik, who took them and piled them in the kitchen. Every once in a while he would run out to the gate. In the back room Silas came upon a leather sack in the corner and dragged it out into the light. It was full of heavy lumps. They opened it and looked inside with curiosity.

"Stones," said Ben-Godik, disappointed. "Then it's nothing."

Silas put his arm into the sack and took something out. He sniffed it and felt it and finally bit it with his teeth.

"It tastes of metal," he said.

"What kind?"

"It's gray—Don't you think it could be ore from the silver mines in the mountains?"

"But they're far away."

Ben-Godik also took out a lump and tried it with his teeth.

"What else could it be?" asked Silas. "I think they steal it and sail it across the water at night."

Ben-Godik lifted the sack and nodded.

"It is heavy, isn't it?"

When the deaf lady came back much later, there was not a trace of their hasty search of her room. The firewood was stacked in place again and the floor swept, and Silas was bounding about intrepidly out in the yard with the horse.

The deaf lady glared at him crossly after that long wait in the shed where of course no one had come.

THREE

The escape

DURING THE DAYS that followed, the deaf woman and the boys kept an equally close watch on each other without discovering anything at all. On the surface everything seemed to be the same as always. Nothing was said.

But every evening Silas and Ben-Godik lay waiting for the stranger to reappear and get more sacks from under the deaf lady's firewood.

Nothing happened.

It was strange, because he had said that he would come for the rest of it. Could it be that in spite of everything the deaf lady had come to suspect that they knew something—and had warned the man? Silas wondered, but they hadn't taken anything from her room and they had put everything back in its proper place again.

Ben-Godik announced that someone snooped around in his things out in the stable from time to time when he wasn't there, and one day it was obvious that someone had been up in the loft.

That same evening there was a tapping on the kitchen window again.

And while the woman was out opening the door, the boys carefully loosened the board and, bursting with curiosity, placed themselves so that they could look down into the kitchen. They really wanted to see what the man was like. But to their great disappointment the deaf lady promptly dragged the man along with her into the cold parlor so they could neither hear nor see what took place.

Right then and there Silas felt that something was wrong and he whispered to Ben-Godik to stay where he was while he, supple as an eel, slipped down the steep stairs to the scullery. But he could not hear anything from in there either; he had to go all the way into the kitchen and so, with incredible caution, he lifted the latch.

It was dark in the kitchen, but a streak of light under the door to the parlor indicated that the deaf lady had taken her taper in there and had not closed the door properly behind her. In fact, because of the strip of light, Silas could make out enough to move around quietly without bumping into anything. By stretching out full length on the floor he could put both eyes and ears to the door opening without being seen, not that this helped very much in terms of seeing the man, for because of the table and the cloth that hung down over it, Silas could see no more of him than a pair of enormous wool socks pulled up over a pair of boots. The deaf lady was already well into a murmured explanation of something or other.

"Four men," she said. "That is plenty."

"Are you sure? We can't have any kind of disturbance."

"Are you grown men or not?" the deaf lady answered scornfully. "They are only a couple of half-grown boys and I say yes, you can take them while they're sleeping —and stuff something down their throats so they can't call out for help."

"After we've got them in the boat, should we throw them overboard when we're under way, or what?"

"For all I care, you can take them with you all the way over there," said the deaf lady. "The main thing is to get them away from here without any fuss. I'm sure they know too much—and over there they won't make any trouble."

Silas felt a cold chill creep right down his spine.

"When?" asked the man.

"It's still too early; wait until later. They should be sleeping heavily."

There was a pause.

"What about the horses?" asked the man guardedly.

"I'll attend to that myself," said the deaf lady unresponsively.

"Kill them?"

"That's up to me."

"If you sell the black, you share what you get," ordered the man.

"Mind your own business," the woman requested. "I'm thinking of sending her out to the gristmill on the river for the miller to resell her. A great many people go there and he has arranged horse sales before."

"He has the best place to hide his stuff anyway," replied the man thoughtfully. "Not even a cat could find a way to crawl in under the water wheel. . . . On the other hand he has so much stored down there that he'd be hung if he were caught."

"So? Wouldn't we all? The point is just to silence those who know too much."

The man in the parlor rose and Silas saw the wool socks move across the floor. As swift as lightning he got to his feet and dashed out into scullery without daring to close the latch behind him. He had to settle for pulling the door to. Soundlessly he scurried up the stairs to the loft and lay down up there. Then the man came out.

"Why the hell didn't you shut the door properly?" he hissed when he touched the latch.

"Shush—"

The deaf lady stood holding her taper and Silas could tell from her tense expression that she knew she had closed it properly.

"Damn it, sloppiness like that," spluttered the man indignantly, "could cost you your head."

Hushing him, the deaf lady bustled him off out into the yard. Afterward she stood for a long time staring thoughtfully at the latch before she went to bed. Only when they finally heard her snore did the boys dare whisper together, and, to be as cautious as the woman downstairs, Silas drew Ben-Godik with him clear across to the other end of the loft and let him know what their prospects were for that night.

"We have to get away from here immediately," explained Silas. He pulled his bedding out of the tent and started rolling it up in the dark.

"What about the horses?" asked Ben-Godik hesitantly, rolling his up too. Silas stashed their savings in his clothes.

"Yours is to be killed," he said.

"And yours?"

"Sold to some damn miller."

Ben-Godik was silent awhile.

Then he asked, "What about the wood carving?"

"We have to leave it all. We need the blankets more at this season, and we have to hurry."

"But I want to take my woodwork anyway," Ben-Godik retorted, cutting a big piece out of their tent.

Down below the deaf lady had stopped snoring.

As quietly as possible they began to descend narrow, steep stairs with their few possessions. If only they could reach the stable, they would probably be able to manage the rest.

But even before they got all the way down to the stone floor, the kitchen door opened and the deaf lady appeared dressed in a wool cloak holding her taper. It crossed Silas' mind that she must have been standing there waiting for them.

"Where are you off to?" she asked coldly.

"Out to pee," replied Silas swiftly.

"Do you need your bedclothes for that?"

For the first time she forgot to say, "What?" and to make them shout. The boys took it as an indication of how dangerous the situation was.

"Shouldn't you wait until morning to go your way?

Surely you didn't intend to cheat me out of what you owe me?"

"What do we owe?"

"For the rest of the winter."

"You'll get that in the spring," Silas promised.

"You won't leave here until you pay," threatened the deaf lady.

But both Silas and Ben-Godik were aware that all this was only a pretext to spin out the time to keep them there until the men returned to get them.

"Here it is," said Silas, who stood ahead on the stairs. "Here is your payment." And he shoved her so hard in the chest with his rolled-up blanket that she dropped the taper and stumbled backwards. And before she could manage to regain her balance he propelled her rapidly into the kitchen and slammed the door on her.

The deaf lady screamed and threatened them with all the misfortunes of the country but Silas kept his foot at the bottom of the door and asked Ben-Godik to bring the broom which they wedged in between the door and the stairs to jam it shut. Then they picked up the end of the taper, which was still burning where it lay in a little pool of melted tallow, and they took it with them hastily over to the stable. It made their work with the horses easier.

But while they strapped on their blankets and untied the animals they could hear the old witch swearing and bellowing and pounding on the door with flat smacks of both hands. Ben-Godik swiftly gathered up his woodwork and rolled it into the piece he had cut from the horse blanket and fastened it to the harness.

"I think I hear something," he said, blowing out the taper and stuffing it into his pocket. "I think they're coming."

They both listened, and sure enough someone was rustling around the gate.

"Mount in here," said Silas, hunching over on the mare's back under the rather low roof. Ben-Godik also turned his horse to face the door and mounted. The men were inside the kitchen now and the deaf lady was jabbering away so loudly that they could hear everything she said clear across the yard. She told the men that the boys were in the stable.

"She should have had to sit in there until she withers," muttered Silas between his teeth. "We didn't do anything to her."

Just then one of the men, in stocking feet, dashed across the yard and threw open the stable door.

Silas dug his heels into the mare's flanks and she burst out, while the man tried to grab him and pull him off. But Silas had not trained the mare in vain. All he had to do was jerk the reins and she reared and walked forward fencing with her hooves so that the man had to jump aside in terror.

Ben-Godik followed close behind Silas so as not to be separated from him and when the man had to give up trying to catch Silas, he turned resolutely toward the next rider with his hand out at least to make this one fall off.

Ben-Godik turned Shags toward him and a blessed odor of fish assailed the horse's nose. There was no doubt that the smell came from the outstretched hands, and swift as lightning Shags closed his yellow teeth around the nearest fist of fingers. The man pulled back his hand with a howl of pain.

One of the others strode over to accomplish what the first had not, but he was also clearly a fisherman with the same promising smell and his hand also ended up right in the horse's mouth. After all, neither of them could have known that this particular horse had been fed on fish waste for most of his life.

"Goddamn nag!" shouted the man who had been bitten, holding his fractured fingers while he hopped around the yard.

The deaf lady came rushing out with a storm lantern. "Have you got them?" she shouted.

No one answered.

Now the two of them would surely keep back, thought Ben-Godik, heading his horse for the woman with the lantern. With great gusto Shags gaped toward her in the hope that she too would smell of fish, and in her confusion the deaf lady thrust the lantern forward as if to shield herself with it.

"Thanks," said Ben-Godik, taking it out of her hand.

"Come on!" shouted Silas, who had fought his way clear into the entryway.

Just then one of them grabbed hold of Ben-Godik's sleeve. "I've got him! I've got him!" shouted the voice right in Ben-Godik's ear. Ben-Godik struck his attacker over the head with the lantern so that it went out.

Now one of them grabbed his leg from the other side and two at once were more than he could handle. Ben-Godik let out a yell and clung to the mane with both hands while the two men hauled one in either direction.

40

He called to Silas who was already out on the street. And in the dim light from a dull streetlamp he saw his friend tear at his shirt and grab his flute.

Realizing Silas' intention, Ben-Godik flung himself forward over the horse, hooking his arms down around its neck. The instant Silas blew a shrill note on the flute Shags took off as if shot from a cannon, aiming for the narrow middle section which was the only part of the heavy gate that was open. Silas really knew what he was doing when he enticed that horse with the flute.

The two men who were clinging to either side of Ben-Godik suspected nothing and didn't even have a chance to let go. With a thundering crash they slammed against the closed parts of the gate and were scraped off at once when the horse and Ben-Godik rushed on through the opening. The gate opening had been designed neither for riders nor coach drivers but only for individuals on foot. A farmer riding a stocky farm horse would have had a terrible job squeezing through.

Beyond lay the street and the night, and Silas and Ben-Godik didn't linger to hear what became of the two men inside the gate. They scarcely had to touch their horses with their heels, for both the mare and Shags had been so riled by the scuffle that they instantly broke into a gallop of their own accord and thundered so hard down the streets toward the outskirts of town that sparks flew from the uneven cobbles. Now it was simply a matter of being able to escape before the shamed and bitten fishermen could call out to the town guards to close the town gates. Four bashed and shattered men in one night were not likely to pass unnoticed.

Even if the boys wanted to tell the truth, who would

believe them? No one would believe that the deaf lady was not really even the slightest bit deaf—anyone would certainly be convinced by talking with her that she didn't hear a thing—and those who lived near her could testify that she'd been like that for years. . . . No, the only thing to do was get as far away as possible before it was too late.

All through the night they rode and it was well into the next day before they began to look around for a place to halt and rest both themselves and the horses. They had deliberately chosen a deserted part of the country to conceal their flight, but now it was almost too much of a good thing, for a long time passed before they finally caught sight of anything resembling a house. Even then what they finally found did not look particularly promising.

They stood still out on the road for a long time looking in through the thick hedge at something not much like an ordinary dwelling, more like a stable with small, semicircular peepholes. But there was a chimney at any rate—and smoke coming out of it. So there was also bound to be someone inside.

FOUR

Jef

RESOLUTELY SILAS PRESSED the mare on through a hole in the hedge and, followed by Ben-Godik, found a footpath of sorts leading in toward the house. Branches and shrubs brushed against them from either side and both of them puzzled separately over what kind of people would live in such a place. They could not be farmers, for there were no fields, only woods on one side of the tangled, overgrown garden and desolate open spaces on the other.

Silas dismounted and knocked firmly on the door. A child's terrified face appeared in a peephole and then vanished. No one opened the door.

Silas waited awhile. Now they had seen that someone was inside. Then he knocked again.

Not a sound could be heard from within the house.

43

"He is frightened," Ben-Godik explained quietly.

"Was it a boy—with all that hair?"

"It doesn't matter," said Ben-Godik. "Just open up," he shouted louder. "We won't do anything to you."

The heavy, warped plank door creaked open a crack and an anxious, timid eye came into view under a wild bush of hair.

"Come on out," said Ben-Godik in a friendly way. "We won't do anything."

The child opened the door quite a bit more.

"I'm not allowed to."

"Why not?"

Deep silence from within the murkiness.

"What's your name?" asked Silas.

And this time the answer came promptly.

"I'm called Jonah and she is my grandmother."

"Good heavens," Silas burst out in surprise, "we know you. You were with a big black lady."

"Yes," said the boy, and they could hear from his voice that he remembered them, too.

"Why don't you come out?"

"I'm not allowed to talk to anyone."

"Why not?"

"Because no one is to know who I am."

"But you've already gone and told us that your name is Jonah and that she's your grandmother."

"That is something she has told me to say."

"Then what is your name?"

"Jef."

"Isn't she home?" Silas nodded in toward the room behind the boy.

The boy shook his head.

"Do you think we could have permission to stay here tonight?"

The boy looked mortally terrified at the thought.

"I'm not allowed to open the door to anyone," he whispered.

"But what if we say that we just walked right in?"

The boy hesitated.

"After all, we could just walk in and wait for her. When will she come home?"

"I don't know."

"Well then, where is she?"

"She never says where she's going. She just goes."

"Then we'll stay here until she comes," decided Silas, tying his horse to an apple tree. Ben-Godik tethered his to another. Inside the door they stopped for a moment and looked around while their eyes became accustomed to the dim light. The peepholes did not let in much daylight and the fire in the hearth at the gable end of the house consisted only of glowing embers. All the same they immediately felt that this was a remarkable house. Even the smell inside.

There was only this one room, and it had obviously been a stable originally—remains of the stalls still jutted out from the back wall and the floor was a stable floor laid with flat fieldstones. Only the fireplace with its attached chimney had been added on later. At the opposite end lay a large, deep pile of straw, that was all. Not so much as a table or chair was to be seen anywhere; the only thing that resembled furniture in the slightest was the green pushcart sitting in state in the corner just

45

inside the door, and the only thing resembling a partition was a thick wall of stacked firewood separating the straw pile from the hearth.

In the middle of the straw lay a huge and not particularly clean quilt, there were no sheets in sight and the coarse quilt was shiny from grease and covered with food stains. In the most remote corner lay a ragged collection of blankets.

"Do you live here all the time?" asked Silas, walking over to warm himself by the fire. It was good to come into a house after the long hours outside.

"Only in the winter," said Jef.

"But if she isn't your grandmother, who is she?" asked Ben-Godik.

"I don't know," replied Jef timidly. "They call her the Horse Crone when she can't hear them."

"Who?"

"People—People she sharpens for."

"Sharpens?"

"Knives and things like that." Jef pointed to the corner where the grindstone stood in her pushcart. "She's a knife-grinder."

"But if you live with her you must know who she is," Silas exclaimed.

"No," said Jef. "She just came and took me suddenly."

"Took you how?" Silas grew more and more astonished.

"On the beach," replied Jef, "right in front of my father's house."

"Where was that?"

"I don't know; it was in the spring—the plovers had just come."

Over by the hearth Ben-Godik laid a log on the embers so that the fire blazed up and began sending out warmth into the room.

"What do you eat in this house?" he asked. "I can't recall the last time I was so starved."

Jef hesitated.

"This is all I have," he said, taking out a couple of lopsided, hard lumps of bread from a hiding place in the woodpile. "They're not very good, but they're the best I can bake."

He shyly offered a gray hunk to each of them, and it seemed to please him that both Ben-Godik and Silas munched away with ravenous appetites.

"Couldn't we give the horses a little of that?" said Ben-Godik afterward, kicking the straw pile.

Jef opened his mouth to protest but immediately closed it again. He had already done so much that was wrong that a little straw more or less wouldn't make much difference.

"How did she happen to take you?" asked Silas later. And Jef told them how he had been sitting on a beach not very far from home and had seen her coming. A big black person right at the water's edge and he was staring so hard that he had forgotten the stones and shells that he was holding.

"She could have been a man," he said. "Even close up, she looked like a man except for the skirt flopping around her ankles.

"Sometimes the water came all the way up over her boots," he said. And they could hear from the trembling in his voice how he had sat motionless, almost paralyzed, watching her come.

47

"Her head looked like a pipefish," said Jef.

"What's that?" asked Ben-Godik.

"That's a thin fish with a long snout that you catch in seaweed in the summer."

He paused, but neither Silas nor Ben-Godik knew anything about what lived in the sea.

And Jef said that just as she was passing him she leaned down, grabbed his arm hard, and without stopping an instant she pulled him to his feet and dragged him off with her. It had all happened so fast that he had not even thought of running away.

"Come along," was all she had said.

And he had bobbed up and down in protest and tried to wriggle free but she just closed her fingers tighter around his arm and turned her hideous face threateningly toward him until he fell silent. And by then they were so far from his father's house that no one would have been able to hear him anymore. Everything would have been drowned out in the heavy crash of waves against the shore if he had called out. And his resistance had dissolved into black, mute terror.

The strangers sat motionless each on a piece of firewood listening to Jef, and Jef felt unable to stop his words. It had been so long since he had had anyone to talk with and he talked and talked and couldn't stop. Now he needed to tell it all.

She had dragged him along with her down the beach all that day, he said; only when it finally got dark and had been dark for quite a while did she stop, but then in any case he didn't know where he was anymore. For a while they had slept on a fishnet in a boathouse, and he was freezing cold even though she had lit a fire in the

48

middle of the floor. And early the next morning there was a ferry dock and a kind of ferryman and some other people who also wanted to be sailed across, and the boat had been full of baskets and bundles that they wanted with them.

"Why didn't you tell them that she had taken you?" asked Silas.

Jef shook his head.

"She was squeezing me so hard. And when we were going to the boat she said that my name was Jonah and that she was my grandmother.

" 'You're called Jonah and I'm your grandmother, you remember that,' she said."

Jef told how he had tried to protest that he was not Jonah and that he would much prefer to be home. He had a grandmother already and he didn't want to sail away.

Her bony fingers had closed tighter and tighter around him until he shut up and was Jonah with a pipefish for a grandmother. And on the other side of the water the knife-grinding pushcart stood waiting and she immediately put the harness on his back and over his shoulders and told him to pull it and soon after that it was she who gave him food and told him where to sleep.

He had pulled and pulled the cart and his name had been Jonah all summer and almost all autumn and she didn't have to tie him to her wrist at night anymore because he would never have been able to find his way home again.

When they came to a house she would walk in and ask for knives and scissors and he discovered that everyone was a little frightened of her. There was also that strong, rank smell hanging about her that made chickens and dogs clear away from her when she came near. It was her eyes, people said. It was her smell, Jef thought. And Silas and Ben-Godik nodded.

When the weather turned cold and windy they had come to this house and Jef had not known that it belonged to the knife-grinder. She had lowered the handles on the cart so that the legs dug into the gravel on the road and then she left it standing there while she went inside to look around.

The door had not been locked. And she shoved it open with such vehemence that there was not a shred of doubt that this was her property. Jef had felt that it was her house, and her door and that she had the right to wrench it off the wall if she felt like it.

The heavy door had been flung all the way back against the wall with a bang and stayed there; the hole it left behind gaped black and stuffy, and it swallowed the knife-grinder like an open mouth. Jef stood outside where the dry leaves on the trees made a melancholy rustling and he heard her move around in the darkness.

It was the Horse Crone's house, and she had groped her way to the hearth at the far end where she found a long wood shingle which she lit. And with the long shingle lifted high she studied the roof and the walls and kicked about in a flattened pile of rotten straw. Jef had not wanted to stay there even for one night—and now he had stayed there all winter.

"Some firewood is down under there," she had said, pointing to the straw. "Look around for it all the way back to the wall."

She had turned with the lit shingle and swept the old ashes to one side of the hearth with the edge of her hand which she then wiped on her skirt. Jef had stayed just inside the door as if he had not heard anything she said. Exhaustion sat like a dead weight on his limbs and he was freezing cold and famished. And it wasn't even a real house that they had come to.

"Well, damn it, spread out that straw and find the wood, before you fall asleep."

The knife-grinder's laughing voice sent Jef right into the unappetizing straw pile as if she had landed a blow on the back of his neck; he had leaped for his life, groped about in the scraps of straw as best he could, his body crouching, his stiff fingers, weak from exposure to the cold, fumbling unhelpfully. His chest made him cough and cough.

"Get on with it!" she ordered from the hearth. "I want logs."

Jef coughed. Never before and never since then had he coughed as he did in all the muck and dust he stirred up that evening. In the dark, blindly, he had dug his way down to the logs and chucked them out onto the floor while weeping and cursing soundlessly.

What a rathole, what a dung heap, what a loathsome, disgusting, ill-natured witch, shrew, pipefish, crow, horse crone, whose only thought was to kill him. She could get her own firewood if she wanted it so badly; she could cough her own lungs out, but he was always the one who had to do things like this.

The picture of Jef chucking the firewood out of the straw became clear to Silas and Ben-Godik as he told them how he had cried and hawked and spat and how he had known that he was supposed to die from it, to rot from all the dust that got inside him. He thought at the time that he was bound to die that very night—he'd freeze to death; it was as cold in there as it was under the ground.

And they understood that in the midst of all that misery Jef's one satisfaction had been that the Horse Crone would have to pull her own cart in the future. It had remained standing out on the road and he couldn't have cared less.

Over on the hearth the knife-grinder had laid a fire and lit it, and from some secret place in her chimney she had taken out a pan. And when the logs were burning nicely she went out to the road and wheeled the cart in, over to the fire where there was a corner just right for it.

Silas and Ben-Godik turned their heads to look at it.

"That cart has lots of room," said Jef. "Everything can fit in it, dead chickens, bacon, and bread." He went over and opened the covering doors of the green storage cupboard to show them.

And she had fetched something from there and tossed it into the pan and a warm smell of frying had filled the room. And the dust had instantly settled and Jef stopped coughing. Nor was he hungry anymore after that, and much against his will he had slept through the night without freezing and without dying from the terrible treatment he had received. And Jef realized that this was where she usually spent the winter. Every winter. He could tell that from the straw—it was more than used; she had completely slept it to pieces by lying on it for years until it looked like gray chaff.

"It doesn't look like gray chaff now," said Silas.

"We changed it," said Jef. "When I woke that first morning, she was standing eating with her back against the wall. She turned her head just as I opened my eyes as if she could hear them open.

" 'You can throw that out on the rubbish heap,' she said pointing at me with a piece of white meat.

"I didn't know what she meant. She ate the meat and then wiped her fingers on the bottom of her skirt, opened the door, closed it behind her, and was gone."

"She left?" asked Ben-Godik in astonishment.

"When I looked out the peephole I couldn't see her and when I went outside she was gone. I ran all the way out to the road."

And the others heard from his voice what that had been like for him, how his arms had drooped in despair, and how he had been startled by the sound of something running. Shuffling, sneaking.

It was withered leaves on the road.

All the withered leaves were skipping along the road with light, shuffling feet. There was not a trace of the Horse Crone.

"I thought she would never come back," said Jef quietly. "I thought she had gone—forever.

" 'Throw that out,' she had said. I didn't know what I was supposed to throw out, because there was nothing in here but the straw. Was that it? I had to go back in the house so as not to freeze."

"And then you carried out the straw?" asked Silas.

Jef nodded.

"I had to do that to make her come back again."

"And did she come?"

"Not right away. I carried all of it over to where there once was a rubbish heap, and the wind skipped around with it and spread it out over the whole garden and right out onto the road and afterward I swept the floor with some branches. She hadn't told me to do that, but it was so she would come back. I swept all the stones. And I swept the ashes together in the fireplace, swept the dust down from the walls—they had been white once but they weren't really very white anymore—and the spider webs from the windows. And finally there wasn't anything else to sweep."

"Then what did you do?"

"Put more wood on the fire and sat down and waited. And I wasn't the one who was crying—I'm sure I wasn't the one who was crying—it was something that I could hear. There was someone crying so loudly that I didn't hear her at all until she was back—not until she opened the door with a bang and was angry. That was because she thought I was the one crying. She hunched in through the door with a mighty load of straw on her back.

" 'Stop that sniveling!' she shouted, 'and spread this out over there.' And then she threw it all down on the floor and went out again and I couldn't hear any more blubbering. It was like a big bundle of sunshine.

"After that she went to the well and tasted the water. It was her own water and that was the first day. And she went around from tree to tree, biting into

54

the windfall fruit and into fruit still hanging on the branches. It was her orchard. Finally she went into the woods that were growing into the orchard. They were her woods and she looked at the trees and when she came back from that walk she found an ax and a saw up in the loft and brought them down.

" 'We'll start in the morning,' was all she said."

Jef told them that he had not known what they were going to start, but the next morning she took him in among the trees. Walking along with the large ax over her shoulder she resembled a man more than ever, and more than ever she was silent and powerful. For hours Jef hung on the other end of the saw and let himself be pulled back and forth, wondering how she could possibly imagine that he was sawing in any way at all.

But she pulled her end and said nothing. And she carried the logs home while he tagged along with little sticks. And by the time the deep frost came half the house was filled with firewood that had not been aged so that it sparked and spat when you put it on the fire. Not very much of it was left now.

And one day she came with a sack of flour. Another day with a barrel of salted meat on her back, then with an armload of smoked sausages to hang in the chimney. Jef asked no questions.

One day she came home with a quilt.

"Put something on the fire," she had said, and Jef had put more logs on while she kicked her own ragged blankets over to his place and spread out the quilt.

"Cook some porridge," she ordered.

Jef obediently cooked some porridge even though he

55

had never tried to before, while the Horse Crone sat down beside the quilt and patted it the way you pat a dog.

Jef served her the porridge where she was sitting, and little by little as the day went by the knife-grinder moved further and further in under the big quilt as if it were eating her up.

"And the next morning she didn't get up," he said.

"Was she ill?" asked Silas.

"She just slept," said Jef.

"Like a bear," said Ben-Godik with a smile.

"She lay there all winter," Jef explained, "though she did eat whatever I gave her."

"But where is she now?"

"She went off; she never says where she's going or how long she'll be away."

Silas and Ben-Godik sat silently for a long time thinking about what Jef had told them.

Then Silas asked, "What is the name of the town you came from?"

"It wasn't a town," replied Jef. "Just some houses."

"What was the water you sailed over?"

"I don't know."

"Was it the ocean or a river?"

"I don't know because it was so cold, but it didn't take so very long and you could see the opposite shore all the time."

"We might be able to take you home," Ben-Godik proposed.

Jef straightened up with a start and looked around wildly.

"Listen!"

The others didn't think that they heard anything.

"Here she comes," whispered Jef, his face growing tense.

They all turned simultaneously toward the door which crashed open as if a bull had run into it from outside.

FIVE

The Horse Crone

THE KNIFE-GRINDER stopped just inside the door and everything in the house fell silent. Even the fire stopped crackling and crouched silently waiting for whatever would happen. The effect of the mighty bang of the door was tremendous in the ensuing silence, during which the towering dark woman just stood there looking around her house with a wary expression.

Silas stared at her undaunted, and in the reddish glow from the fire she looked even more fantastic than he remembered. Shadows underlined the long hollows beneath her prominent cheekbones and her chin jutted out sharply. But it was more than that. Something emanated from her, a kind of madness streamed out of her body with that rank smell and made her awesome. There was no doubt that she would be capable of absolutely anything, and Silas felt in his stomach why Jef was so frightened of her.

A pipefish, he thought, a pipefish looks like this?

But when she opened her mouth, her voice at any rate was not like a pipefish's. No fish could sound like that and still be a fish. Her voice grated like a file against a saw blade, a very forceful, raw iron sound; it went right through your clothes and rang on your skin like a shivery chill, while her dangerous eyes slowly shifted from Jef to the strangers and from them back to Jef again. He lowered his head guiltily and seemed to become smaller and smaller under her terrible gaze.

"Well?"

Her voice nailed him to the floor.

"I see you're entertaining guests."

Jef hunched down guiltily and denied nothing.

"Who are they?"

Without taking her eyes from Jef, the knife-grinder pointed to Silas and Ben-Godik with one of the fingers that had dragged Jef away from his home.

Jef's face turned white. The rest of him had almost vanished from terror, for after all he didn't even know who they were, only that he had seen them on the street and that they had been friendly. And now he had gone and opened the door for them and told them everything that he was not allowed to tell a soul.

"Damn it, Jonah, answer me—"

Her voice echoed under the roof and Jef shrank as if she had struck him with a whip.

"I—I don't know," he sobbed out almost inaudibly, "just some people who came."

Silas hunched down and tensed his legs ready to

spring between them if she should try to lay a hand on the poor boy.

"We walked in ourselves," he said clearly.

A touch of surprise appeared in her enraged face. "Did someone say something?"

"We would like to stay here tonight," Silas went on before she could pull herself together.

"Do you think I'm running a roadside inn for vagabonds?" she almost shouted without budging from the wide-open doorway. "What a pack of thieves."

Both Silas and Ben-Godik stood up and protested.

The Horse Crone just looked at them and a malicious grin settled around her mouth making her enormous teeth protrude. Her hard eyes did not smile.

"Go on, tell me," she said, "where a couple of pups like you could get a horse like that—short of stealing her." She turned part way to point—just in time to catch sight of Shags, who was hurrying toward her with his muzzle extended and who calmly began to nibble up and down her back with every indication of delight.

The knife-grinder punched him between the eyes with her clenched fist and he looked at her reproachfully through the partings in his forelock.

Shags had grown bored with being tethered and had tugged so long at the reins that he had got loose and aimed straight for the opening in the side of the house. Ben-Godik ran over and stopped him from entering; Silas hurried out to see to the black mare.

"I won her in a wager," he explained in passing.

"Is that so?" said the knife-grinder, not believing him.

"What about this little fellow?"

60

"We borrowed him."

The Horse Crone pulled a wry face again.

"You expect me to believe that?"

She walked over to the mare. Ben-Godik hastily hung Shags' reins over a branch and went along too.

"No," said Silas. "I don't care what you believe— but we don't have a place to sleep and we would really fancy having an omelet with pork and fried potatoes this evening."

The knife-grinder turned toward him abruptly; her evaluating glance wandered up and down his not particularly well-dressed person.

Then she said, "That depends on whether you can pay for it."

Ben-Godik watched her closely. He saw something happen under those wisps of hair covered by that hat. Behind their backs Shags sneaked away from the branch and stole over toward the door again. Seeing him come, Jef turned weak at the knees, for he was frightened of horses and didn't dare touch him or chase him out—and after having got so out of favor with the Horse Crone, he didn't dare appeal to her either. The less she was made aware of his presence the better. So instead he pressed himself flat against the wall and let the animal pass him, after which he dashed out and stood over by the gable end of the house.

It was cowardly of him, he knew that perfectly well, but what could he do. Over by the mare he could hear that they were discussing money.

"A sack of silver ore," he heard Silas say.

Jef didn't know what silver ore was, but he understood from the tone of voice—and from the knife-grinder's watchful, suspicious attitude—that it was something rather special.

He could hear the horse rummaging around inside the house. It rattled the pot hanging over the fire, snuffled in the ashes and sneezed, and began to gnaw on something or other. Jef guessed that it was the crusty remains of the porridge inside the pot. That was what they would have had themselves for dinner, by warming it up with a little water to stir it soft again. He didn't dare even peek once around the corner to see what mischief the horse was up to.

Over by the other horse the conversation had sunk to a muted murmur, they were negotiating something or other, he thought.

In the house, Shags was wandering around sniffing the floor. Jef could hear him rooting about in the straw for a long while, then there was silence. More silence than he cared to hear.

"Jonah!" the knife-grinder bellowed suddenly.

Jef started.

"Come over here, boy, when I talk to you."

Jef shuffled away from his hiding place despondently and then stopped.

"Fry up some meat and potatoes."

The knife-grinder's voice sounded excited as if she had just made a good transaction—or else intended to.

Jef stopped indecisively by the door not daring to go inside. Just then Ben-Godik noticed that his horse had disappeared again. He looked over at Jef.

"Where did he go?"

"In there—"

Jef's eyes became excessively large in his terrified little face but it seemed as if Ben-Godik had expected that very answer for he was already on his way over toward the entrance.

The knife-grinder threw a dirty look at the boy by the door and Jef lowered his eyes. He was well aware that it was his fault.

"There's no horse here," Ben-Godik's voice sounded from within the semidarkness. He came back out again.

"I saw him go in," whispered Jef.

They all went in to have a look. The horse was nowhere to be seen. Ben-Godik was apparently right—until the knife-grinder let out a bellow.

"Hell's bells—my quilt—it's ruined!"

Neither Silas nor Ben-Godik had paid particular attention to the great number of feathers wafting around over the floor inside the door, since there was so much other dirt and dust lying about. Now they looked at the straw pile—it was all mottled with chicken feathers and every step they took stirred up the down.

The knife-grinder swore miserably.

"But where is the horse?" asked Ben-Godik anxiously. As far as he could see there was no other door.

"There," said Silas, pointing to the feathers.

The others said nothing and Ben-Godik thought that he was fooling him.

"There," repeated Silas, pointing. And through a hole in the pile of feathers beamed one of Shags' eyes. He had burrowed down in the hollow in the straw where the knife-grinder had slept all winter and in so doing he had made a hole in the quilt.

"You'll pay for this," swore the knife-grinder angrily, not addressing anyone in particular. Or at least Silas was not sure whether she meant him or the horse.

"Well, he was freezing cold," he said casually.

"But he doesn't have to destroy other people's furniture," the knife-grinder pointed out.

"What if there happened to be two sacks of silver ore instead of one?" said Silas in his wiliest and most captivating voice. "Then surely there would be enough for a quilt as well as our lodgings for the night."

"You and your silver ore—you and your sacks— If you think I'm taken in by everything you tell me, you're mistaken. . . . And if you think that I'll fill you with food for having been taken in—"

The knife-grinder sneezed. She was really seriously furious now because of the quilt and she had forgotten that she had just shouted to Jef to fry meat and potatoes.

"You'll get the address after we've eaten," Silas reminded her of their agreement.

"Like hell I'll feed you," she hissed.

"But you said that you—"

"I'll keep the horse as security while you fetch the sacks. I'd say that's a much better arrangement."

The knife-grinder shoved her hideous face at Silas and blew her bad breath into his face while she impaled his eyes on hers. Silas had to control himself so as not to make a face; he tried to stop breathing instead.

"What about him, then?" he asked, pointing to Ben-Godik.

"He can stay here and work for his supper in the meantime," came the prompt reply.

Shuddering at the thought, Ben-Godik hauled the horse up out of the straw and led him back outside.

"So then it's settled," said Silas.

The knife-grinder glared at him in surprise; she had not expected such compliance. She had thought that he was lying, she really hadn't believed any of his talk about the sacks—he didn't even want to say where they were.

Jef fried the meat.

Now and then he glanced over his shoulder. The knife-grinder sat beating eggs in a wooden bowl with the sad remains of her only ladle. Shags had appropriated it while he was attending to the remains of the porridge in the pot. Her threatening expression when she found out that it had been destroyed elicited an immediate promise from Ben-Godik to make her a new one, and now he was sitting whittling behind her back. From time to time she would glance at his quick hands in much the same way that Jef glanced at the bowl she sat holding. It was a long time since they had had a meal with eggs.

When the meat was ready he fished it out onto a board and sliced pieces of potato into the bubbling fat in the pan. She had not told him how to go about it, but he thought this was probably all right, though he still expected to be struck in the back by her bellows of protest at any moment. This made all his movements nervous; he jumped at the slightest sound.

But nothing happened. The whole house was more wonderfully peaceful than he had ever known it. The boys were silent from hunger, and the Horse Crone was full of new and remarkable thoughts. When the glow from the fire flickered over her face he could see that she was working her jaws and knitting her brows together over a distant and inward expression.

And the peace continued. Jef felt such anxiety in his body that he thought he might burst from it, for he knew the Horse Crone well enough to know that when she was gentle and quiet, something was wrong. That was when she was busy plotting something—but how could he warn the strangers about the danger if he himself did not know what she was plotting?

He jumped when she asked whether the potatoes were tender yet. "Yes," he whispered, poking them with the tip of a knife. Forks did not exist in that household. "Yes."

The Horse Crone flung the batch of eggs into the sizzling fat so that they popped and crackled, and from some hidden recess between the ceiling and the wall she fetched a jug of ale. The sight of that reinforced Jef's belief in her evil intentions and he turned in torment toward Ben-Godik without knowing what he should say.

"Well, here's your food!" shouted the knife-grinder.

Silas and Ben-Godik came over and watched in amazement as that bony person cut the omelet dexterously into four pieces with the knife and placed each portion tidily on a piece of split wood. Perfectly ordinary pieces of firewood. That way they could make do without plates and she kept her melted fat in the pan for later.

"Here," she said, handing each of them a well-heaped piece of wood. How to go about eating the sizzling hot, steaming mass each had to work out for himself; for her part she sat down by one corner of the woodpile placing her food on her skirts, the knife in her right hand, grasping a big piece of fried pork in her left. The others falteringly followed her example and, with grease dripping on their thighs, speared the omelet piece by piece and stuck it in their mouths, while they loudly praised the food. Seldom had a meal tasted so good, they said.

Both the Horse Crone and Jef raked in the praise separately and after the meal the mood was very contented. Jef hoped that this might last through the night and that he had been mistaken about the knife-grinder's silence. Quiet as a shadow he crept softly around the hearth, clearing up and putting things away in their proper places, while the other three fell back into the straw to digest.

But no sooner had the Horse Crone placed herself in the midst of the feathers than she demanded the address of the house where the silver ore was stashed in sacks.

"But you agreed that I would go get it myself," protested Silas, lazily picking his teeth with a piece of straw.

"That's why I really ought to know where it is."

"Wait until tomorrow morning," murmured Silas. He noticed that the ale had made him sleepy.

"No," commanded the knife-grinder sharply.

Jef laid the greasy pieces of wood on top of the fire and for a while the room became brighter.

"In that case I want both horses in here tonight," Silas demanded in return. "I can't bear it that they're just standing outside."

The knife-grinder yelled angrily that she would not permit such big animals in her living room, and Silas suppressed a wry smile at her description.

But after a while she added that he could put them in a shed out back. She had a shed, and if a little space were cleared in it they could certainly stay there.

They talked back and forth about it and Ben-Godik said that he wanted to go out and see what it was like.

"Then come back with an answer," ordered the knife-grinder.

Silas laughed. For all he cared she might as well know where the silver was to be found; he was not involved in any part of it and not pledged to silence in any way.

"Then why didn't you take it yourself?"

"What could I have done with it? Do you think I care to drag around sacks as heavy as a load of stones?"

"But since it's silver?"

"They're still just as heavy," asserted Silas. He wondered vaguely why Ben-Godik had not come back.

"Then where are they?"

"In town we lived in a house owned by an old deaf lady in Fisherman Street," Silas began.

"Where you lived is beside the point. What do I care?" interrupted the knife-grinder impatiently.

"An old deaf woman," Silas went on.

"Yes, thank you, I know her well. No matter how loud I shout, it's impossible to make her understand the price of sharpening a very ordinary bread knife. She will only pay half."

"She can hear perfectly well," chuckled Silas.

"Can she indeed? She's deaf as a post and dumb as a shovel."

"She is not deaf," Silas insisted.

"Well, she's been like that for many years," the knife-grinder assured him. "She lost her hearing a long time ago."

"Then try pulling a pair of wool socks over your boots," said Silas.

The knife-grinder swung her head toward him irascibly.

"Why should I do that?"

"And sneak into her yard one dark night," Silas went on.

"Stop all this nonsense," commanded the knife-grinder. "If you think you can talk yourself out of it this way, you're wrong. Come to the point. Why should I care about the deaf woman and her backyard?"

"And tap on her kitchen window with one of your long dirty fingernails," said Silas.

"I asked you, what does the deaf woman have to do with it all?" said the enraged knife-grinder. "Why should I do that? Such tomfoolery!"

"She's the one who has it," said Silas.

The enormous woman sat up with a jolt and clapped her hat in place on her hair.

"You want me to believe that?" she shrilled scornfully.

"I lived in the loft right over her most of the winter."

"What of it? What does that have to do with it?"

"There was a peephole down into the kitchen," said Silas, giving a huge yawn.

"Are you trying to convince me that she has silver in her kitchen?"

"No," said Silas.

"Well?"

"In the room off it. Under the firewood."

The knife-grinder studied him at length, with every sign of distrust.

"That is by far the worst I have heard in a long time," she muttered, flopping back into the straw so that the feathers rose up around her in a cloud. "And to top it all off, now I'll have to freeze in my own house," she added with a grumble.

They could hear Ben-Godik rummaging around out back moving things out. It took a long time. Then there was silence but still a long time passed before he came back in.

"That certainly took time," murmured Silas when the other finally appeared with a blanket under each arm.

"A big load of junk had to be moved first," replied Ben-Godik. "Two whole horses take up a lot of space."

"Could you lock up properly?" Silas wanted to know.

"Yes," said Ben-Godik.

"How?" asked the knife-grinder with interest. "There's no latch anymore."

"A pole on an angle is something they can't move from inside," Ben Godik explained. "They won't run off anywhere tonight."

The knife-grinder smiled sarcastically and lay down to snore. Jef had long since cuddled up in his ragged collection of blankets and not long passed before Silas also fell asleep.

But Ben-Godik was awake. Still as a mouse he lay listening and before very long it turned out that his suspicions proved to be well-founded. The knife-grinder raised herself up carefully and he could hear her listening to the sounds of the sleepers. Cautiously she pushed her way out of the straw and crept over to the door, which she didn't scrape over the floor as usual but instead lifted it open quietly and, when she had gone out, lifted it again until she had closed it equally quietly. Shortly afterward Ben-Godik could see her contour silhouetted against the night sky. She was wearing her hat and her coachman's cape.

She went around behind the house.

Ben-Godik stretched out his arm and woke Silas.

"What is it?"

"We have to go out now—quickly."

Silas instantly gathered that something was wrong and pulled his blanket with him out onto the floor.

Ben-Godik touched Jef and woke him.

"Get up and come with us," he whispered.

Groggy with sleep, Jef protested, but Ben-Godik took him by the wrist and pulled him along. Out back they could hear rummaging and heavy thuds.

Silas tensed, listening.

"The horses!"

He was already on his way toward the door at top speed to prevent the knife-grinder from making off with their animals.

"No," Ben-Godik exclaimed, grabbing him by the belt. "They're not there."

"Where are they?" Silas was alarmed and angry.

"Hush," whispered Ben-Godik, easing the door open just enough for them to slip out.

"Can you find the path to the road?" he said into Jef's ear but Jef only whimpered and didn't answer.

71

"Shush," whispered Ben-Godik harshly. "If she finds us she'll kill us."

The little fellow immediately stopped. Ben-Godik pulled him along anyway and also found something that he thought was the path.

They were almost out of the garden when the knife-grinder came around the corner, her skirts lashing her legs, and disappeared inside her door.

"Now she's seen that they're not there," breathed Ben-Godik.

"Lie down," commanded Silas from behind, flattening himself as far in under a bush as he could. A second later the knife-grinder's boots stormed by going toward the road which she surveyed some distance in both directions. Not a horse or boy in sight. But she had not heard them ride off—they couldn't be far away yet. She stormed around in the back garden, beginning her search for them there.

"Now!" said Ben-Godik.

With Jef between them and the blankets flapping loosely over their shoulders, they ran out onto the road and a good way into the woods. There in a clearing stood both horses surrounded by thick underbrush so that they could not be seen from the road; the black mare with her reins around a young tree and Shags secured to a rusty cow tether that rattled whenever it moved.

"It was lying around in the shed, so I thought I might as well make good use of it," explained Ben-Godik, happy that they had got away.

"How did you know that she wanted to steal them?" asked Silas.

"This young fellow gave me a warning signal," said Ben-Godik, clapping Jef on the shoulder in a friendly way.

"But I didn't say anything," said Jef in astonishment. "I didn't have any idea what would happen."

"No, but I could see from you that something was wrong, so I put the horses here for safety's sake. I mean —when you told her straight out where the silver sacks were couldn't you see the greedy look in her eyes?—and what is the quickest way to leave a place where there are a couple of horses?"

"Then what was she doing out there in the shed?" Silas wanted to know.

"She couldn't get in. I piled all her own mess together right in front of the door, so she had to move that first."

From inside the knife-grinder's house came a crash informing them that she had kicked the door. Jef started. He knew that sound all too well.

"Now she's very, very furious," he said in a low voice, looking in the direction of the house. "She always kicks when she's in that kind of mood." Jef shuddered from the cold and fear.

"Well," Silas suggested, "don't you worry about that now; she has other things besides you to think about at the moment. You just come along with us. Two of us can ride my horse perfectly well."

To his great surprise Jef started to cry.

"Why are you blubbering?" asked Silas. "Would you rather stay here?"

Jef hesitated.

"I don't dare," he sniffled.

"What don't you dare?"

"Ride."

"Are you scared of her?" Silas pointed to the mare. Jef just nodded.

Silas took him by the hand and led him over right in front of the big black animal. "Come here so that she can say hello to you," he said.

Jef went along reluctantly.

"Say hello to Jef," Silas ordered. And the mare lifted one foreleg and offered it to him.

"Now you," he said to Jef, who took hold of the hoof anxiously.

"Now give her this."

Silas put something in Jef's palm and guided his hand toward the big head even though Jef struggled against him.

The mare sniffed and tickled Jef's palm with the soft hairs on her muzzle while she carefully took the crusts of bread with her lips.

"That was some of what you baked yourself," said Silas. "Now you can surely ride her."

Very impressed, Jef looked from the horse down to his hand as if he had never seen any of its parts before, and Silas untied the reins and helped him up onto the horse's high back. Then he himself leaped up and hung his blanket around the boy's shoulders in front of him. The sky was gray with the approaching dawn.

From inside the knife-grinder's house came the sound of the heavy pushcart being bumped over the threshold and the sound of the stout plank door being slammed shut.

"Now she's off," said Jef, listening.

"Now we ride," said Silas. And off they rode.

74

SIX

The farmer with the big ax

LATE ONE EVENING they stopped at a small farm set somewhat off by itself. There was no light anywhere and neither Silas nor Ben-Godik cared to rouse anyone just to ask permission to sleep in the barn, for that would probably have been refused. No one liked to be awakened for so little.

But since there was no other place with lights to be seen in the vicinity, they decided to stay where they were and find a place to sleep on their own.

Behind the dung heap a couple of trees and some shrubs had taken root, and there they tied the horses so that they could not be seen as clearly is if they were standing right out in the open. Then the three boys crept cautiously along the barn wall around the farmyard to where Silas eased open the door of the cow barn. A

75

marvelous, warm, cozy, and welcoming vapor greeted them and they really felt how much they needed rest and sleep.

"Don't close the latch," warned Silas. "That makes a noise, and we'll be off early in the morning before anyone hears us."

Jef, who came last, did as he was told, contenting himself with simply pulling the door to. A faint smell of beets blended with the sweet scent of cows and Ben-Godik wished that they could find some kohlrabi that was not rotten or damaged by frost, not likely at that season. They stopped just inside the door, partly to accustom their eyes to the darkness and partly so as not to frighten the cows into making a noise, but the animals immediately noticed that strangers had come in anyway and stirred uneasily.

"There are no empty stalls here," murmured Silas quietly. "These must be good times for this farmer with such a full barn."

"I'm sure there's plenty of room in the hayloft," Ben-Godik said, looking around for a hole through which they could climb.

"There's a ladder," whispered Jef eagerly, happy to be of some use. "Over on the other side of the cows," he added, pointing over to the feed alley.

The ladder was quite narrow, pieced together with thin stripped spruce branches, but there was no doubt that it led up to the hayloft, and the boys groped their way in single file past the row of standing or lying cows, who stuck big, long-horned heads out through their halters and slobberingly sniffed at their feet as they passed. The feed alley was not particularly wide;

76

Jef pressed back against the outer wall anxiously and held Ben-Godik's sleeve tightly when he had to pass a cow with unusually long horns.

"They won't do anything," Ben-Godik assured him. "They're just curious."

Jef stifled a howl when a rough, wet cow's tongue suddenly licked his knee.

"Hush!"

Silas was already on the ladder with his head up through the hole.

"It's as black up here as inside a whale's stomach," he announced.

"That doesn't matter; we have Jonah with us," murmured Ben-Godik.

"We'll have to feel our way," came from above, as Silas disappeared from the edge of the hole on his hands and knees. "Don't walk too heavily," he said, "or your legs will go through."

It was not as warm up in the hayloft as down in the cow barn and they spread one blanket on the hay for all three of them to lie on, pulled the other over them, and heaped a thick layer of hay on top. That way they were fine. And they fell swiftly asleep to the peaceful sound of the creatures munching away down in the barn, everything breathing contentedly, while occasionally a cow would rub its horn against the woodwork or make a noisy plop in the dung channel.

But later in the night they were abruptly roused from their good sleep by a terrible din. The cows bellowed and butted the woodwork so that the whole building shook, and there was a restless stampeding of many feet down below, a heaving and turning of large bodies as if they were all milling around each other in great agitation. The boys up in the loft sat still as mice listening for a second. Then Silas wriggled on his stomach over to the edge of the hole and looked down. A faint grayish light had begun to seep in down there and he could just make out that only one of the cows had got loose and that she was wandering merrily back and forth behind the others, who were all kicking and tugging at their halters to get free.

Up in the hay the others held their breath and waited for an explanation. It was impossible for them to figure out what had happened.

An unmistakable, suppressed curse from Silas, who was still hanging over the edge of the hole with his head in the space below, made them start.

"It's the horse," he said over his shoulder.

He had to crawl down using a windowsill and the front edge of a stall, because the cows had knocked over the ladder by wildly swinging their horns back and forth. The whole building was rocking and boiling over with all the animals pulling at their tethers.

Jef and Ben-Godik crawled over and peered down. Shags was walking back and forth behind the cows planting his probing teeth into anything that protruded. The handle of the thresher had already been planed down to wood shavings and he was now at work on the cows' bony backsides. Such a long row of tails could only be sticking out there to be tugged, and it was all the more fun whenever an owner let out a bellow and banged her head against a post. Shags looked as if he was having a fine time.

Silas went toward him cursing and raging but actually he was having a hard time keeping serious, for the horse swung his head around, stared out at him through his straggling mane, and laughed—a high, bubbling laugh that started way down in his stomach and finally came out between his teeth. Silas reached him in a second.

"No-good critter," he scolded, grabbing him by the forelock.

The horse nodded, showing not a trace of guilt.

"You could have broken their tails," Silas went on. "Then what do you think the farmer would have said?"

Shags shook his head to get free from his hand.

"You're the freshest creature that's ever been stuffed into a horse's hide," he continued, gathering up the loose ends of the reins. "It would have made more sense if you'd been born with only three legs—that would have been plenty for you. Just look at what you've done now. . . . Monster."

He held the broken ends of the reins right under Shags' nose accusingly. They had trailed back and forth across the barn floor and were wet and slippery with cow dung.

"First you gnaw these as if you were a puppy not a horse, then you torment these sober citizens. What a wretch you are. Shame on you!"

Silas stopped and tied the ends of the reins together. The horse turned its head toward him as if to fathom his mood. Right in front of Shags' nose hung a cow's tail, as tempting as the bellpull on a burgher's front door. And before Silas realized what he was thinking of, Shags had pulled the bell and let go again. The cow sounded like a fire alarm and the horse turned his head again and peeked out slyly through his forelock at Silas.

Silas sighed in resignation.

"Bring my blanket down with you," he called to the hole in the loft. "We must be off now. It's getting light out."

Ben-Godik crawled down the way he had watched Silas do it and then he put the ladder up for Jef, and Silas led Shags over toward the door holding the bridle firmly. The barn door stood almost wide open now; it was not the horse's habit to close a door behind him.

Right outside stood the farmer barring the way with a huge ax in his hand.

Silas stopped abruptly and pushed Shags back into the barn. A deadly weapon like that could split even the sturdiest work horse's forehead as if it were nothing.

"Damn thieving knave!" shouted the farmer, jumping up and down in his wooden clogs, which were very new and rather big in contrast to the rest of his otherwise wizened and bandy-legged appearance.

"Were you going to steal my cows?"

"No," said Silas from within the barn's darkness. Neither he nor the others had thought of stealing anything at all.

"Come out here!" ordered the farmer shrilly. "I'll see to you."

Silas hung back unobtrusively.

"Let go of that cow and come out here," said the farmer.

"It's not a cow, it's a horse," Silas told him.

"Nonsense. Don't you think I know what I have in my own barn?"

The man outside rocked up and down on his bowed knees, swinging the ax back and forth down over the ground as if he were about to fell a big tree. The sight gave Silas a nasty dread that his ankles would be chopped off. Perhaps the farmer intended to hack off his feet.

"Don't you think I know what sort of fellow you are?" the man went on shouting, his gaze boring into the darkness inside the barn. "Do you think I've already forgotten how you took two calves from here last week? But it's all over now, you know, now I've got you— come on out."

In spite of his small size, he wielded his tremendous implement with the dexterity of a practiced woodsman, and Silas stayed wisely inside the threshold.

"Let go of my cow," said the man.

Out of a door from someplace Silas could not see quietly came a thin, agitated female figure in her shift, and shortly after there appeared an overgrown youth who looked obviously like their legitimate offspring. The woman clasped her shift anxiously around her throat at the sight of the man swinging the ax; she didn't dare come close enough to see what was really happening. But the son opened his sleep-bleary eyes very wide and raked one hand through his mop of hair, which stood out in all directions like yellow bracken. He was much bigger than his father and much clumsier. Silas thought he seemed slow and heavy and was not really frightened of him.

The farmer gave the son an order to go in and take the cow away from Silas. The son approached, shilly-shallying, then hunched down to look in through the door. Silas drew back with Shags.

"What cow?" asked the son, not understanding, from his bent-over position.

"The one he's standing with, you blockhead," spluttered the father, hopping up and down in his clogs. "The one he was about to steal, what else?"

"It's not a cow, it's a horse," said the son.

The farmer gave his son a wise look. Then he approached on his bent knees and peered intently into the darkness that was steadily growing paler in the early light. As for the ax, he held that up carefully in front of his face with one eye on either side of the blade. It poked out from his forehead and extended all the way down to cover his chin like a big, sharp nose. He was truly not someone to joke with.

Silas dragged Shags out so that the farmer could really see that it was a horse and not a cow, as he had maintained. And Silas was in no doubt that the farmer had discovered his mistake, for his face came to look completely different behind the ax. Some time passed before he said anything, and Silas got the uncomfortable feeling that the man was up to something. And he was right.

For the third time the farmer said to his son to go in and take the cow from the thief.

But now Silas protested loudly.

"Or you won't get out of this alive," said the farmer, standing rigid, gesticulating with the ax, and Silas realized that the man out there was in the process of forcibly acquiring a free horse. He simply intended to keep it. Inside the barn behind Silas, Ben-Godik grumbled threateningly. As for the horse, he leaned forward staring intently at the ax. Silas smiled to himself, well aware of what Shags desired.

"Let go," ordered the farmer sharply.

His intention was clear enough. The son was to grab hold of the horse and the farmer would chase the alleged cattle thieves out of the farmyard.

Silas did as he ordered and let go of the bridle.

And the son stepped forward to grab Shags. But neither father nor son could have suspected what sort of animal they had before them. The beast aimed straight for the shiny, handmade shaft of the farmer's ax, not to be stopped just because someone happened to be there with outstretched arms. Instead, the horse stepped meticulously upon the young man's toes as he pushed past him in the direction of the farmer.

Following Shags, Silas was able to walk out unhindered into the farmyard where the son was hopping on one leg, holding the other foot. Even Jef and Ben-Godik came out into the light now. Involuntarily the farmer stepped back when he saw the horse's bared yellow teeth coming right at him. And even though he already considered the horse his own property, it didn't occur to him to strike it on the forehead with his ax; instead he fended it off with his elbow.

But to his astonishment he discovered that he wasn't what the horse was after; it snapped at the shiny smooth ax shaft instead and he hastily hid the tool behind his back.

Thrusting both hands in his pockets, Silas relished

83

this priceless scene. They looked as if they were dancing around each other, the farmer keeping the ax behind his back all the while and Shags nipping his sleeves to make him produce that delectable shaft again.

But the farmer was not of a mind to let it get hold of the ax; an ax was something that he could not do without, and Silas could tell from the shaft which was nearly black from wear and sweat that it had probably belonged to both the farmer's father and grandfather.

"Do your cows always do this?" laughed Silas.

The farmer snarled like a dog.

"I think it seems quite hungry," Silas went on. "Perhaps you give it too little food."

The farmer scowled. It was obvious that he couldn't manage very much longer.

"Come on and help, you dunce!" he shrieked to the son, who was hobbling over.

"Grab hold of him," said the father.

The son dutifully put his arms around Shags' neck and leaned forward over the horse, prepared to give his all for his hard-pressed father. But now that was just too much for the horse. With a couple of irascible head tosses, Shags broke free, smashing his head against the son's in the process so that the latter slid soundlessly to the ground.

Silas leaned contentedly against the wall.

"I've never seen a cow like that before," he said. "Will you try milking her?"

But the farmer was not going to listen to any more. The son was stretched out full length on the ground, of no further use, and the crazy horse was all over him again to get the ax handle. Giving up, the little, shriveled farmer made a sudden leap out of his wooden clogs, dashed over to the scullery door and in to his wife, who had removed herself from the scene some time before.

Shags was right at his heels but the farmer slammed the door and the horse, snorting in disappointment, nosed around the door behind which he had disappeared.

"No roast joint of ax today," said Silas from over by the wall.

Turning his head to look at him, Shags also caught sight of the farmer's abandoned wooden clogs alone in the middle of the farmyard. The tall, unconscious figure beside them did not concern him at all, but such big, new clogs were truly not to be despised—especially with straw in them. Shags poked his muzzle down into one and blew. Then he took hold of one with his teeth and went over to Silas.

Ben-Godik wanted to take the clog away from him, but Silas said that he thought the horse should keep it. It wasn't really very much considering what he had saved them from.

The dismayed faces of the man and his wife appeared at the window; Silas thought that they were probably frightened that someone would harm their son. But why would they do that? They were not violent ruffians, not even cattle thieves; they had just slept in the hayloft overnight. They rolled up their blankets and set off around the barn, only to discover when they arrived out back that the mare was gone.

For a second they stood completely still unable to believe it. On one tree were the remains of the reins that

Shags had gnawed through, on the other tree there was nothing.

"That was what he came to tell us last night," said Ben-Godik.

"Shags?"

Ben-Godik nodded. "But by then it was probably already too late," he said.

"Do you think the farmer could have moved her before he came to the barn door with the ax?" asked Silas.

Jef noticed something on the ground.

"Look there!" he shouted.

The others did not understand what he meant right away; there was nothing but pungent, wet, and somewhat broken up earth and manure.

"The boots!" cried Jef.

Silas sighed, what good were boot tracks. But Jef was not going to stop again; he tramped around in the sludgy mud staring at the ground and ended way over where the shrubbery was very thick. Then he let out a triumphant shout.

"Her cart was here!" he called out.

"Whose?"

"The Horse Crone's pushcart." Already noticeably subdued, Jef reemerged from the underbrush, as if a thought had struck him. He looked sadly at Shags, who was standing munching the clog with relish and spitting the splinters out onto the ground. The Horse Crone was the most powerful and most dangerous person he knew.

"We have to go after her," cried Silas.

Jef began to weep very quietly.

"What is it now?" asked Silas. "You don't have to

blubber just because you catch sight of her cart. She's far away."

"It's not that," sobbed Jef. "I don't like staying here when he has an ax like that."

"Staying here?" Both Silas and Ben-Godik turned to him in surprise. "Who said you're going to stay here?"

"Well, since you only have one horse now—and only two can sit on him."

"Only one of us will ride," said Ben-Godik, "and he's the one." He pointed to Silas.

Jef gaped. The tears had drawn stripes in the dust from the hayloft. "Why?"

"Because he has to hurry," said Ben-Godik.

Silas was already out on the road looking for the mare's tracks to find the right direction. Ben-Godik tied one blanket onto the horse and made Jef hold the other. Then he leaned down over what was left of the farmer's chewed clog, and took the iron clamps out of it, carefully collected all the nails, and put them in his pocket.

"What do you want them for?" asked Jef.

"I don't know."

"Then why are you taking them?"

"You can always find some use for a nail." Ben-Godik led the horse out onto the road where Silas had finished his investigations.

The two bigger boys looked at each other.

"We can take care of ourselves," said Ben-Godik, seeing the other's concerned expression. "We'll ask the way. You just get going."

Silas hesitated. What had begun so accidentally in the field where Ben-Godik was tending the town cows, had since then turned into friendship. In all the time that had passed neither of them had thought about that, for they had been together all the time, but now that they suddenly couldn't be together anymore, they were aware of it. But Ben-Godik was right. If he wanted to get his mare back, he would have to follow the tracks swiftly.

Silent and determined, he rode away following the tracks without knowing where they were leading him.

SEVEN

The fire

SILAS RODE HARD.

All that first day he was sure that he wanted to overtake the knife-grinder quickly, and her audacity made him seethe with anger and indignation. For he was in no doubt that she had snatched the horse so that she could reach the town more quickly—hadn't he himself told her where the deaf lady hid her silver?

But gradually as he followed her tracks he became more and more perplexed, for they led away from the town. What did she intend to do here—and what was she doing with a horse?

The first stretch from the farm she had ridden at a gallop, he could tell. Later, she took it more peacefully, letting the mare trot, but when Silas hadn't caught up with her the next day either, he realized that she was traveling at a good clip toward a very definite destination. The tracks were still there and it seemed as if this strange dark female knew the district with unerring certainty, for she zigzagged her way ahead by the most deserted and desolate places.

But why was she avoiding houses? And why did she make such wide detours? A less observant pursuer would have long since lost her tracks.

Silas pressed both himself and Shags as much as he dared, resting only when the horse had to rest and eating only when the horse had to have food. His eyes sank into his head from fatigue and lack of sleep, but still he had to go on, all the time further on, even though he knew that he could not overtake the mare on this horse.

That very first morning he had crossed a fairly substantial stream not too far from the angry farmer's property. Even at the ford the current was powerful and the river surged a good way up Shags' belly and Silas had concluded that he would come to the river soon. But how surprised he was when instead he reached a long, narrow lake surrounded by high hills.

Right where the stream emptied into the long lake stood a cluster of houses, but Silas knew from the start that it was pointless to ask for the knife-grinder there, because the tracks already led on over the hills, following a path around the lake along the crest of the hills.

Silas could not stop imagining how she must have looked from the houses down below, a black flapping figure on a black horse. Like an evil portent she had crossed the skyline with her skirts flapping behind her, perhaps a portent of approaching plague or bad times.

It had struck him that he himself could be seen just

as clearly—a half-grown boy on a short-legged, long-haired horse. How would he be interpreted?

He brooded over this while he rode the rest of the day alongside the narrow lake, always high up with a view over the water across to the opposite shore and, on his shore, over sandy, rolling country. No one lived there and the exposed character of the place made him wakeful and watchful in spite of his exhausted state. Not a crow escaped his glance, not a single yellow bunting.

Over on the opposite shore boats lay pulled up among the reeds and out in the lake in several places were posts with eel traps and markers for fishing lines with bottom hooks. Over there were houses.

Silas had lived on beets and carrots and whatever else he could find for so long that the thought of a fish made his mouth water. His stomach grumbled and if there had been some way for him to get out to the reeds, he would have done so.

But when, just before nightfall, he reached the other end of the long lake, he did catch sight of something after all. Between the hills and the water was a flat stretch of land with some trees on it, and around where the lake dwindled into a river stood something resembling a heather roof placed directly on the ground.

Silas stopped. But if somewhere in his empty stomach he had hopes that people lived in that strange structure, maybe even people who would be willing to give him something to eat, he was sadly mistaken. The house was empty. And it was nothing more than a heather roof standing right on the earth. He shoved open the door and looked in. It was where the boat was supposed to stay in winter, the boat that was presently rocking about in the reeds. The door was as wide as a smallish gate, but at the same time low, and inside the hut there was plenty of room and not too much to see. Only a small assortment of fishing tackle hanging all the way over on the back wall.

Silas searched through things not knowing what they were used for and found something that he thought must be a hand-fishing line. There was a hook and a little metal weight on one end of the line, and although Silas had never done very much fishing he knew enough that if you had a hook you had to have some bait.

He took the line down from the wall and tried it in his hand. Then he went out and kicked up the earth behind the hut to find a worm. A big, fat beetle grub turned up in the hole and Silas hesitated slightly. Could that be used? He had never heard of anyone fishing with grubs. There were no worms to be seen and his stomach growled persistently, so he put the grub on the hook and swung his leg into the boat and stood up in the stern with the coiled line in one hand and the end with the hook dangling from his other hand. The rising hills circling the lake seemed to continue down under the surface of the water with the same steepness and the lake looked as if it reached a great depth precipitously.

That was good because then there was a chance for a bite down there.

Very carefully Silas swung the hook with the grub on it around a couple of times and then let go, convinced that the line would fly out in a perfect arc, causing the hook to land suitably far out in the water.

And it did go very well to begin with. The sinker

pulled the line with it out of his left hand in the right sequence—until suddenly there wasn't any order left and all the rest plopped out among the reeds in a mess of loops and knots.

Silas competed with his stomach in grumbling and began to haul in the line bit by bit, disentangling it gradually, which was fairly difficult considering that the fading daylight was already well mixed with beginning twilight. In between the knots he glanced at the sky, which was clear and green out toward the west. He would have to hurry if he wanted food before he lay down to sleep.

The boat rocked peacefully among the reeds while he undid the knots as hard as he could—or left them if they were completely hopeless. Without warning the line was suddenly wrenched out of his fingers with a sharp tug and the already nicely untangled line whipped out of the boat again at a furious pace. For a second Silas stared dumbfounded as his tidily coiled line leaped from the boat and whizzed out into the lake. Then he grabbed the gunwale with one hand and hung over it with all his weight. A singeing burn spread right across his palm until the line finally came to a stop.

With his free hand he wound the remaining length around the oarlock a couple of times and secured it with a clove hitch. It all happened so fast that he didn't even have time to think; he only finally came to himself when the line stretched taut and straight as a steel wire from the gunwale, describing figure eights on the surface of the water.

Could it be a fish?

Feeling the torn flesh on his palm, Silas became quite

alarmed. Without touching the line he considered what it might be. What would live in the bottom of such a lake? It could have pulled him in over the gunwale. He shuddered. Then he pulled himself together, planted his feet firmly against the ribs of the boat's hull, and hauled in the line with both hands. The boat bobbed and splashed up and down.

Silas looked over his shoulder. The skiff had come free from the bank where the prow had been beached conveniently; now it was on its way out into the lake after the fish. And the plucky fisherman could only choose between jumping overboard while he could still touch bottom or staying where he was—naturally there were no oars.

Land a fish or not?

Were he to jump off, the fish would tire itself out swimming and give up and die and he would not get the slightest benefit from it—nor have any possibility of catching another. So he stayed.

The fish pulled very silently out toward the middle of the lake while the darkness around him grew deeper and deeper. A long time passed before the fish was so exhausted that it let itself be hauled up to the surface, and it was even longer before he managed to get this adversary into the boat without falling into the water himself in the process. But he had never seen—or more accurately felt, since he could not see anything any longer—a fish like this before. Covered with bumps and scars and obviously ancient, it lay slapping its tail in the bilge water. Even being in the boat with it was a risky undertaking. He knew that he had to kill it. Its jaws were full of teeth—that he had noticed—and were it to grab a finger, there was no knowing how much he would have left for himself.

Silas pulled out his long knife, leaned toward the tail and felt his way up from there to the back of its neck. That was where he knew you were supposed to cut in. But before he managed to sink the blade in, the fish struck at his wet trouser leg with its teeth and clamped its jaws shut. In panic Silas sliced into its neck, a big, deep cut, but it still lashed its tail and he had to wrench himself free from its teeth with his knife blade. It ought to be dead, but he almost cut off its head anyway and tethered it to the floorboards by driving his knife through its gills to skewer it down. Now at least it would stay in the stern.

Silas knelt down right in the bow and began to paddle the icy water with his arms. He barely moved the boat; it took an eternity to get to where the current finally helped him. Shuddering from the cold, his fingers refusing to obey, he wrenched the hook out of the creature's jaws as it lay quite peacefully now and he pulled his knife out and stuck it in the sheath. His sleeves dripping and his arms dead all the way up to his shoulders, he dragged the fish behind him over the gunwale and swung his legs over onto the shore.

He had to have a fire and he had to have one quickly or he would freeze to death. The green evening sky had promised a cold night and, wet as he was, he would not be able to survive without heat. Silas staggered around blindly after fallen branches and other things he could burn, and everything he found he dragged in to the turf hut's earth floor. In there he wanted to light a fire; the roof would hold the heat in around him and no strangers could see his fire.

But it was terribly difficult for him to get it lit when he finally thought that he had piled up enough firewood. His fingers were still stiff and numb after their long stay under water; they wouldn't do what he wanted. When at last he succeeded in catching a spark on a tuft of moss and got it to burn, he watched over it as if it were the world's costliest treasure. The interior of the hut came into view in the faint reddish glow, and it was as if he had gotten his eyes back. Only when he was absolutely sure that the fire was burning properly did he dare go out to find and clean the fish which he had left somewhere between the hut and the boat.

The fish was not there.

He opened the door all the way so that the firelight would fall out in a broad beam, but even so he saw no fish, and no matter how thoroughly he felt around on the ground beyond the light he still did not find it.

An uneasy feeling came over him. What exactly had he caught anyway—and what's more, was it really truly dead? Could it have gone back to the water?

The disappointment over not getting any food after all that trouble was so intense that it affected him almost like paralysis. Silas didn't know how long he stood there in the dark with his arms dangling, not caring that the wind blasted him to the very bones. He just stared at the smooth, silent lake, disheartened and more famished than he could remember ever having been before.

That was when he heard a crunch a short distance away in the blackness—a munching crunch. With an indignant roar he followed the sound and bumped right into Shags. With trembling fingers he fumbled his way to the horse's head, grabbed it by the ear, while with his other hand he felt down over its nose and caught hold of the fish's tail. The head and top half of the fish were already in a chewed consistency in the animal's throat.

Not letting go of the tail and cursing for dear life, Silas pounded his clenched fist against the horse's hard forehead with no real effect. Shags just closed his teeth even tighter around what he had and with a snapping bite broke the fish in two. Silas stood holding his part in his hand.

But he noticed that there was still plenty left for him. It must have been an enormous fish. He went down and scraped the tail clean and hurried in and skewered it on a branch over the fire, while the horse chewed and smacked its lips behind him in the dark. No sooner had Shags swallowed the last morsels than he stood in the open doorway sniffing in toward the speckled tail with extended nostrils. Silas had to close the door and make a smoke hole higher up.

Later he ate and went right on eating until he was absolutely sure that he couldn't stuff down even the tiniest bit more. And all that time the nag stood out there breathing longingly around the edges of the door.

"Go lie down, you greedy bag of bones," he said loudly. "You've had plenty."

Shags didn't budge. The delicious aroma wafting out with the smoke kept him there, and although he had just threatened him, Silas got up and handed a shred of the charred fish skin to the horse outside, sincerely grateful that he had got the hook out before he dropped the fish on the ground. Then he took his blanket and made himself comfortable on the earth floor beside the fire. A good night's sleep would not be amiss now, he thought.

But a good night's sleep was apparently not what he was to have. His fire burned down and he woke freezing and stood up dazed with sleep and threw on more firewood, a lot more wood; he wanted to be able to sleep right through until morning. Then he lay down again —until the horse outside woke him with a shrill whinny.

Silas sat up with a jolt, a sharp light and intense heat closed in around him. The hut was on fire. The whole end with the door was enveloped in flames; he couldn't get out that way. Outside the horse screamed again and in one leap Silas was on his feet. With his knife in his hand he attacked the back wall, slashing and sawing into the tight willow wattle and the entwined straw ropes that secured the turf roof in place. The heat scorched his back; he hacked and sawed without making any progress—and all the while the fire ate its way closer to him. Unbelievably strong and tightly made this wretched hut was; desperately he bashed at the solid back wall and when it finally gave way, both his clothes and his hair were in flames.

Without thinking twice and without so much as dropping the knife, he ran around the hut and dashed right out into the black, flame-reflecting water which closed over him with a bubbling fizz. It was like being burned again; Silas could not endure it—like a cat he shot right back out on shore again. The heat was awesomely intense now, the hut stood like a flaming tent of fire, and steam rose like white smoke from his wet clothes. His hair did not smell good and the skin on his back stung; nevertheless he stayed as close to the heat as possible to get dry. Not until the wood frame crashed down in flames did he jump out of the way. A column of sparks rose up between the trees and sank back down again into a glowing heap on the ground. He stared silently at the hut that was no longer there—and the sky was red and gray from the coming day.

When it got lighter Silas took off his clothes to see how everything looked. His tunic had burned to shreds on his back—and his shirt as well. His flute dropped to the ground. He had forgotten it what with everything else; it had been with him in the fire and out in the lake's icy water. He picked it up carefully and put it to the test at his lips.

And from high up in the hills Shags answered with a long whinny. He had apparently seen to it that he got himself to safety.

Silas put his shirt back on. He noticed that there were blisters on his shoulders. Then he turned the tunic around, buttoning it up the back so as not to have all the holes in the same places. He felt up in his hair. On one side of his head his hair was only an inch long and full of sweaty, black, singed spikes that broke off when he touched them. On the other side his hair came down over his ears. He couldn't look like that. Resolutely he took the knife and cut the hair all over his head to a thumb-length long, and while he was doing it he noticed how the remaining hair rose from the roots relieved of the weight. It made him feel quite different and lighter.

Then he took a last look at the black, collapsed heap before scrambling up to the horse. But Shags refused to recognize him: showing the whites of his eyes, he drew back on stiff legs whenever Silas approached, and Silas had to coax him for a long time with the flute before he overcame his terror of the smell of fire on Silas' body and came close enough for Silas to get hold of him.

Up on the ridge of the hills the tracks of the black mare led on, and for a long time he followed the water, which had turned into a stream once again. Then he came to the big river. And just where the stream emptied into the river stood a house. Not by the side of the stream as he had first assumed, but straddling the river so that the water could flow into a stone chamber under the gristmill's wheel when the grain was being milled and could be diverted when the mill was idle.

Silas studied this strange building a long time, then he hid the horse in a dense thicket as close to the mouth of the stream as possible, where no one could see him from the bridle path above. And, crouching low, he crept stealthily toward the building down at the water's edge.

The gristmill by the river, the deaf lady had said.

This was it.

EIGHT

What took place at the gristmill

SILAS CRAWLED.

The sluice gate was down, the mill was not in use, and, apart from the overflow water falling from the dammed stream down into a deep, stone-lined channel roaring out under the mill building, everything was quiet. Not a person in sight—not even down by the houses further along the road.

And yet Silas found it most advisable not to stand up. Crawling on all fours through the growth of various kinds of low shrubs ringing the mill dam, he approached the large, two-storied wooden building that rested on a massive foundation of granite boulder stonework. The mill blocked off one whole end of the dam, and to flow beyond it the stream had to either tumble down into a gigantic stone chamber directly under the millworks and drive the big waterwheel around, or, as on this day, fall pell-mell into the overflow channel.

Right by the mill Silas crawled in under the exterior footbridge from which the sluice gate could be raised, but he was none the wiser for sitting there. And even though there did prove to be a little narrow door into the millhouse from the footbridge, he could clearly see that that was not the way for him to enter. He had to go around the house, preferably all the way around to the back, so as not to be surprised by someone from the road. He could hear nothing because of the constantly falling water; that ceaseless roar beat at his ears. Silas slipped quietly up onto the footbridge and, still crawling on all fours to avoid the windows, followed it around the corner until he could stand up and teeter on along on a stone-covered part that separated the overflow channel from the mill-wheel chamber. He headed away from the mill in the direction of the river.

He had to walk carefully. It was not a place where anyone would choose to walk; big and little stones lay there all strewn together, and up through the holes protruded broad dock leaves, making it impossible to see where to put your feet. Here someone could break a leg very easily—and be left lying there, and on either side was a deep drop if he should stumble. To one side the powerful whirlpools of the swirling current, to the other the empty stone chamber extending under the wheel where the water would rush in when the mill was working.

Silas looked over the edge. It was far down; it would take at least three men standing on each other's shoulders to reach the top from down there. A couple of little puddles covered some of the bottom, but otherwise it was open under the wheel, a big dark hole in which he could just make out the curve of that gigantic wheel.

Full of curiosity, he slid down over the edge and, with the agility of a lizard, felt his way down the vertical wall for places to grip with his fingers and toes between the not-too-regular stones.

Inside next to the wheel there was more space than there had appeared to be from above: a man could easily move around if it had to be inspected or repaired. Nevertheless he couldn't help imagining what would happen if someone should raise the sluice gate so that the water would come and the wheel start turning while he was standing down there. No one would ever know that he was there, no one would hear if he shouted, and his remains would be carried away by the current out into the river.

And the water certainly was eager to come. High up there he could see it seeping in through leaky places in the sluice gate and falling the long way down with a hollow well-like splash. Somewhere or other up there was the footbridge under which he had sat a short while before.

No one had heard him; no one knew he was there; at any moment the miller might come and raise his sluice gate and start to work. Silas was asking for trouble but still he had to go further into the wet darkness, all the way in behind the deadly dangerous wheel. And in there his foot stumbled against something hard.

Silas leaned over and felt around with his hand. It was a leather sack. He lifted it, lifted up one end, and dropped it again. The sack was slimy wet and heavy as

103

if it were full of stones. He felt with his hand, found more sacks. . . . So she had been right after all, the deaf lady.

Silas left the sacks where they were; it was not silver he was after—it was a horse. The black mare was worth more to him than dangerous sacks of stolen goods. He turned toward the daylight again, but on the way past the wheel his shoulder struck a flat iron ring set into the stone wall. He had not noticed it on his way in but now he looked up and caught sight of several more, arranged one above the other like rungs of a ladder.

Of course, he thought. The miller and his people certainly wouldn't crawl down the sheer wall out back; they would go up and down this way when they wanted to have a look at the wheel—or the sacks. Even though he could not see it, he was convinced that there was someone above him—no one but he would take it into his head to risk life and limb in the stone chamber.

From up inside the mill came the sound of a thud and of someone tramping across the floor in wooden clogs: someone was talking.

Silas did not wait to hear what was being said; he rushed out and up onto the surface of the earth again, but this time on the opposite side of the chamber where he took cover under the dock leaves and weeds in order to sneak around to the front where a shed roof jutted out. It was there that wagons came carrying sacks to be unloaded.

Silas had hoped that he could hear who was talking in the mill from there and perhaps what was being discussed as well but instead it seemed to him that the

104

voices had become more indistinct. Only a faint murmur suggested that someone was even inside the mill.

The door into the mill stood open. Silas crawled along under the roof and looked in. There were sacks everywhere, stacked up against the walls and all around the floor in different piles, but there was not a soul to be seen.

Soundlessly he slipped in behind a pile of sacks. Someone was still talking on and on. Above him. Silas listened. Beside the millstone itself a stairway led skyward and from the loft further up a square wooden chute came down between the timbers and gears right in the middle of the machinery. It was up there, he supposed, that they poured the grain in. If he stretched a little he could see a partition with a door in it at the top of the stairs.

What if he were to creep up there and listen?

Silas lay there a moment wondering whether it would be all right, and while he listened he let his eyes travel over the interior of the millhouse. It was not as dilapidated inside as it had looked from the outside. Could that be intentional?

Before he decided what to do, the door opened and a man in milling clothes came out into the loft right by the stairs.

"All your palaver won't help you," he said over his shoulder through the door. "It must be another mill."

"Do you deny that this is the river gristmill?" said a voice from inside the room.

A hot pang rushed through Silas. It was she. The Horse Crone. Finally he had caught up with her.

The miller continued across the loft above Silas' head and shortly after came into sight again by the door with a gray stone jug in his hand.

"The deaf one on Fisherman Street sends greetings," said the knife-grinder, appearing.

"What deaf one?" asked the miller, unruffled. "I don't know him."

The knife-grinder arched forward and stuck her bony face right up against the man's eyes as he held the jug.

"*Her*," she corrected him. "She said it was here."

"Oh," said the miller.

"You already knew that."

"Go away, now," said the man impatiently. "I don't want to stand here all day."

The knife-grinder didn't move and the miller shoved her back into the room with the bottom of the jug.

"Are you going to hit me, you wretched mealworm?" she hissed at the rough treatment.

"Sit down and begin from the beginning," said the miller, putting the jug down on a table.

The knife-grinder grumbled but the miller didn't let himself be taken in by that.

"Cheers," he said.

They hadn't closed the door behind them; Silas could hear almost every single word. The knife-grinder tried in every conceivable way to find a crack in the miller's claim that he knew nothing about what she was saying, and he was impressively deft at avoiding the traps she laid for him.

This he has rehearsed before, thought Silas. He's playing a part.

Now and then they drank.

"I don't know that woman," the miller maintained. "Why are you so sure that she was telling the truth?"

"She had to," said the knife-grinder spitefully.

"How so?"

"I held a hot coal from her own stove under the sole of her foot."

That sounded diabolical and Silas could hear right away that the good miller was taken aback.

"Good God," he said, giving himself a shake.

"Quite so," laughed the knife-grinder. "Is it gradually beginning to dawn on you what I mean?"

"Let's drink to that," suggested the miller. "Or were you thinking of scorching me?"

"I almost think you should be hung," said the woman dryly.

"No one is hung for serving aquavit—although it definitely is illegal," said the miller calmly.

"It's a good thing that you have a clear conscience, miller, for tomorrow the bailiff is coming to search your house," announced the knife-grinder, her voice full of insinuation.

The miller stood up so suddenly that the chair tumbled over behind him.

"You're lying—"

The Horse Crone laughed like a man and slapped her thighs with delight.

"Who sent word for the bailiff?" bellowed the miller. "Was it you?"

But the knife-grinder just laughed exultantly and the miller, realizing that he had been tricked, fell silent.

"Well? Out with it, miller. Where do you keep it?"

The miller walked out into the loft and fetched another

jug. He no longer denied anything directly nor did he offer the slightest truthful explanation from what Silas heard. Something crafty had come into his way of beating about the bush, and he kept diligently plying her with more to drink. The Horse Crone brayed with pleasure at having trapped him and drank more aquavit, her voice growing more and more husky and babbling. Silas got the impression that the miller wanted to incapacitate her with the help of drink.

Down behind his sack of flour he considered what he should do now and decided that whatever happened, he did not want to lose sight of her until he got his mare back.

From up in the room came a crash and a heavy thud and the miller muttered contemptuously. A moment later he came quietly out the door and after glancing briefly back over his shoulder, went down the stairs and out under the shed.

So she must have fallen on the floor, thought Silas. The miller had succeeded in his endeavor—and he didn't even seem particularly drunk himself. Silas got up and looked out after him through one of the floury windows and saw the man dressed in white rushing over to the houses further down the road.

At that very moment came a snort and scraping sounds from above him, and Silas hid himself for safety's sake. The Horse Crone came out the door, not staggering and reeling or holding the walls as he had expected, but swiftly, with decisive steps. She started searching feverishly around the loft where the miller had fetched the jugs; she went the whole way around along the eaves— Silas could hear—putting her fingers in all the nooks and crannies. He was absolutely sure that she was after the silver. But the miller's vague hints could be interpreted in so many ways, and now she obviously thought that she had taken him in both with her drunkenness and as to where the silver was.

And she hurried. She obviously intended to clear out before he turned up again.

But Silas could have told her that she wouldn't be able to find what she was looking for up under the eaves. The more she looked the more heated and impetuous her movements became. Things were hauled out and thrown on the floor, tools knocked over or scraped back and forth. Even the grain coffers—she did not stick at moving them too from what he could hear. Silas placed himself right at the foot of the stairs to catch her so that she wouldn't break her neck were she soon to come tumbling down. He really wanted to speak with her first.

And there he stood when she came stomping across the floor above with her skirts swishing around her and her face contorted with rage. For a second she stopped short at the sight of him. She didn't recognize him and Silas suddenly remembered his altered appearance. He had forgotten that his clothes were scorched to rags and that his hair consisted of short, uneven tufts all over his skull. His face was probably sooty too; that he did not know.

The knife-grinder obviously wondered what the appearance of this new individual could mean.

"What do you want?" her iron voice called down to him.

"To fetch the horse," said Silas without blinking.

"What horse?"

Suspicion radiated from her; she had clearly not told anyone that she had arrived on horseback.

"Mine," said Silas. "If you don't need her any longer, I'd like to have her back again."

Gathering recognition loomed dangerously within her; she slid down the stairs and grabbed the back of his neck in a flash. He would never have believed such a big person could exist.

"You miserable liar!" she shrieked, shaking him this way and that. "There weren't any sacks of silver at the deaf woman's house as you said, not even the smallest pouch."

"I dare say they shipped them off," gasped Silas, half-choked.

"Yes, and you already knew it. But I'll teach you to come running with lies like that." She hurled him from her so that he slid far across the floor.

Silas jumped up and shook himself like a dog. She had such strength in her fingers, the odious witch; she had almost squeezed his head off. And she hadn't finished yet. Under full sail she headed for him again— and there was no way out for him.

"Horse!" she shrilled. "Did you say you wanted a horse?"

She grabbed for him with her long bony fingers, but this time Silas was as swift as she. He ducked and swerved to one side and she swept past like an avalanche, pulling everything down off the miller's plank table. She turned toward Silas again furiously but by then he was already sitting like a cat up among the big gear wheels under the loft. There at any rate she couldn't reach him.

110

"We can trade," he said from up there.

"I've traded more than enough with you, you scoundrel."

"Yes, but I know where the miller keeps it."

"What?"

"What you're looking for."

"Then tell me!" screamed the knife-grinder wildly.

"I'll trade it for the horse," replied Silas.

"I'll kill you if you don't tell me."

"First tell me where you put the horse," ordered Silas.

"Lies, lies, you don't know anything. You're just talking hot air the way you did about the deaf woman—lies from start to finish. But just wait, you won't get out of this one."

She headed for the mill machinery menacingly and Silas could see from her swift, dark glances that she was searching for something long with which to knock him down. Disappointment over not finding the silver that she had expected, combined with all the aquavit she had drunk, made her lose control and upset her judgment, and Silas was grateful to the absent miller for not keeping long-handled implements in the building. There were only the railings up to the loft, but they were firmly fixed in place.

Of course she could easily have wrenched them off if she happened to think of it, and Silas kept his eyes averted so as not to draw her attention to something that she could use to her advantage. She was not dead drunk, as the miller had assumed—she had been play-acting—but she was furious because she felt cheated and was ready for anything to get revenge. And the mixture of the miller's aquavit and the sight of Silas was more than she could bear.

From up on his gear wheel he followed her movements warily. The knife-grinder grabbed at different handles in the hope of starting the mill so that Silas would be ground to pulp between the massive, iron-sheathed teeth. And Silas silently thanked the miller's aquavit that she didn't first think to raise the sluice gate.

He cautiously repeated his offer to trade the black mare for as many sacks of silver ore as she could drag away from there somehow or other.

The knife-grinder, gnashing her teeth, grabbed a hammer and hurled it at him. Silas ducked, and the hammer sailed out through a pane of glass in the back wall.

A couple of grain shovels came whizzing through the air almost simultaneously. With a bang the larger one struck a post in the back wall and the scoop broke, the other smashed into a gear wheel and disappeared somewhere in the machinery. Silas hid himself as well as he could behind the vertical shaft of the mill, while tools and spare parts of every sort whizzed past his ears. The furious knife-grinder stripped the miller's shelves relentlessly, even his aquavit jugs and his old white wooden clogs each had a turn up under the loft and down by the back wall. A good many things vanished out through the window and ended up in the tangle of shrubbery outside, and Silas was sure that if this rash, confused person got her hands on him she would choke him to death on the spot or maim the life out of him piece by piece. Her eyes glowed like phosphorus and there was no way that he could have reasoned with her. He had to wait until she had stormed out all her rage.

When there were no more things for her to throw up at him, she ripped the shelves off the walls and heaved them up against the gear wheels with such force that the splintered, broken ends of wood flew out from it like sparks. And she kicked out a whole row of windows facing the mill dam with her boots, not just the glass but the frames and sills as well; it all fell out leaving great gaping holes where before there had been white light and poor visibility through flour-covered glass.

Whole piles of grain sacks were overturned across the floor, tumbling down others in their wake. The knife-grinder grinned grimly. The mill looked as if a tornado had passed through it.

Over by one of the windows she had kicked out, the miller's infuriated face appeared with two other fierce-looking heads beside his. Noticing nothing, the knife-grinder kicked away at one of the sacks until the grain poured out in a golden stream, but Silas hunched down and made himself very small. Now serious things were going to happen, for neither the crazed woman nor the three men seemed in a joking mood.

He couldn't help comparing the Horse Crone with the ax farmer, and even though Shags had managed matters with the man in the farmyard, Silas was still glad that he had hidden the horse so far away that at least the knife-grinder could not vent her spiteful rage on him. It was also good that he was alone, that Jef and Ben-Godik were not with him. Silas had always thought

113

that when the fur starts flying, one person alone has the best chance of making it.

Outside a boat bumped quite softly against the sluice gate.

NINE

The Horse Crone faced with a dilemma

SHE TURNED IN one bound when the door opened and
the three men filled the opening. Her silent, wanton
rampage was punctured in much the same way that
shortly before holes had been made in the sack of grain,
and a broad stream of curses spewed out of her mouth
in the direction of the presumptuous miller who would
not part with his secrets.

The knife-grinder kicked a hole in a new sack to
emphasize her wish to bring the entire mill down upon
their heads.

Silas crouched: no one turned to him; no one paid
any attention to him up there under the loft. With
muscles tensed, he watched and waited for what would
happen now.

The three men made no reply to the knife-grinder's

115

abuse; silently they came toward her from three different angles, one step at a time, threateningly, ineluctably—the sight made Silas shiver. No one was approached that way with good intentions.

The Horse Crone was perfectly aware of that, but she was not one to surrender without resistance. She stood up very straight watching them until they were almost upon her, then she made a quick lunge with her arms to mislead the man nearest her, whereupon, swift as lightning, she kicked the next man in the jaw with the toe of her boot.

There was a dumbfounded break in their attention while the man fell to the floor and laboriously got to his feet again. They were obviously at a loss, first because they were not used to fighting with women, and second because they had never met a woman who started a fight on an equal footing. Quite literally.

Cautiously they closed in around her again. The knife-grinder's mouth was drawn narrow as a line and her eyes were black and wary. The next man who came too close was kicked on his arm.

The three men hesitated.

The knife-grinder's kicking technique surpassed anything they had ever encountered of that sort. She was lightning-fast and in spite of her skirts her reach was enormous.

The whole mill held its breath and lay in wait. Outside the water rushed along in the overflow conduit and the sound came in clearly through the smashed windows. No one noticed that a face appeared in one window for a second and then vanished again; no one heard someone creeping stealthily around the corner on the footbridge. Everything was directed toward the knife-grinder.

The miller grabbed a sack of flour and threw it right at her feet, leaned down, lifted another, and landed it beside the first. The two other men stared at him in astonishment, until it suddenly dawned on them what the miller was in the process of doing. Then they too began to throw sacks right around her legs, so many, one on top of the other, and so close to her body that in a short period of time she could no longer lift her boots over them. In a matter of seconds she was walled-in alive and then they had her.

Grinning, the strangers grabbed the knife-grinder's arms and hauled her on her stomach over the piled-up sacks and out onto the floor, where the miller was standing armed with new sacks which he placed on top of her feet. After that they helped each other cover her entire body until only her head was free and then they took up positions around the prisoner, mocking her.

"Well, now, what was it you wanted?"

The knife-grinder blew into the sand on the floor contemptuously and didn't answer.

"What did you come for?"

They punched the heap of sacks lying there, exhorting her with the tips of their wooden clogs. "Well?"

"You'd better ask him up there," she snarled, trying to turn her head all around so that she could see Silas.

"Is she holy?" one of the men asked the miller cautiously.

"Not that I know of. She can both drink aquavit and swear in the worst way."

"So you don't think we should call a priest?"

117

"Only if you want him to be smashed to smithereens."

"Well, I agree she doesn't look like a saint."

"You fathead," groaned the knife-grinder from under her mountain of grain. "I mean him up there in the gears."

The men turned and caught sight of Silas.

"You'd better come down," said the miller threateningly.

"He's the one who sent me over to the deaf woman," said the knife-grinder. "It's his fault that I'm lying here."

"You needn't have stolen my horse," Silas fired back smartly.

"What kind?" asked the miller, showing interest. "A black one?"

"Yes."

Silas looked down at the miller expectantly. Did he know anything?

"He's the one who was spying on the deaf lady," said the miller between his teeth to the man next to him. "We'll get him too."

And in no time they leaped up into the gearing and dragged Silas down by his legs. They laid him down beside the Horse Crone and piled sacks on top of him too so that he could not move a finger.

"There, you lost your own chance to escape," he said to the woman.

"Did you intend to play the knight in shining armor?" came her scornful reply.

"I would have had to as long as I didn't have my horse."

The knife-grinder made faces at him and the men planted themselves in front of them with crossed arms.

"No one will ever know what became of you," explained the miller. "People who know too much always end up floating away from here in small pieces."

The men moved some sacks around and the miller opened the hatch in the floor. Silas did not have to see down in there; he thought with horror of the enormous waterwheel; he knew exactly how little space there was between the wheel and the wall.

And without further words the miller walked out onto the footbridge and raised the sluice gate so that the damned-up water hurtled down into the stone chamber, striking the paddles of the broad wheel as it fell. A shudder passed through the whole building, the last fragments of glass fell out of the shattered windows and ended up tinkling on the floor, the gears shook and grumbled against each other, the shafts squeaked, and slowly, slowly the heavy machinery started working. The din grew louder and louder and Silas was unable to hear whether or not anything was being said. He only saw that the miller pointed to him and for the first time he regretted that he had refused to let Philip teach him how to swallow swords. What was in store for him now would definitely be much worse.

The two men tied his arms together behind his back and seized his legs and carried him over to the hole in the floor. Silas kept his eyes tight shut. If they had not tied his hands he might have been able to grab one of the iron rings, but hanging with his head down this way, unable to use his arms, he was at their mercy. Right

119

under his face the water rushed by, churning around the thundering wheel.

The men just stood there waiting for a signal from the miller, who was minding his crank handles and keeping his eyes on millworkings to see when they reached their fastest speed of rotation.

That was when the water suddenly stopped flowing.

Baffled, the men stared down into the chamber where the wheel immediately stopped as soon as the water flowed away. Then they turned to the miller accusingly.

"Klummerhas, why didn't you fasten it properly?"

"Fasten what properly?"

"The sluice gate, of course; you realize that it has fallen down."

The miller protested. When he raised his sluice gate it wouldn't fall down by itself. He went out in a huff and raised it again. Once more the stationary wheel began to shudder itself into motion, the mill thundered and groaned under the water pressure, and Silas made a silent wish that the whole building would fall to pieces.

It didn't.

And the men dangled him down into the hole a second time while they kept their eyes on the miller over by the levers.

But this time, too, the sluice gate fell down and the machinery stopped just as the wheel was about to reach its peak of speed.

The miller appeared terrified.

"I have never experienced this before," he whispered. "Something isn't working as usual."

The men glowered at him angrily.

"Of course we know that's because you're frightened,"

they said. "You're a coward. When it comes down to it, you don't dare."

"Then do it yourselves," the miller said in his own defense. "You go out and raise the sluice gate."

The men grumbled and dropped Silas onto the floor. Without a word they walked out onto the footbridge and began struggling together to get the sluice gate up for the third time. This took time as they did not have the miller's crank handle. Meanwhile the miller sat himself down on Silas' back. He didn't dare run any risk. If he were to let the boy get away, he knew that he himself would be chucked into the mill wheel and mashed to pulp.

For the third time the mill shook itself and started and the two men came back in and stood expectantly over by the open hatch with their eyes fixed on the water. The gearing got going and nothing happened. They glanced over at the miller triumphantly, grabbed Silas by the legs again and dragged him over to the edge. The knife-grinder lay as if she were asleep or as if her drunkenness had finally overpowered her.

Silas glanced down for a moment at the swirling mass of water.

The miller nodded.

At that instant the water stopped running. The thundering torrent shrank to the gentle, cellarlike drip and splash which Silas already knew so well.

The three men stared at each other speechlessly, then they looked at Silas and from him down into the empty hole.

"Do you—do you think it's because—" whispered the miller, his face as white as the clothes he wore.

"Hush," said one of the others. "Someone is down there—listen."

Quite right. Gradually, as the gearing creaked to a halt, a hollow, ghostlike voice could be heard between the wet stone walls.

"It is *he*," whispered the miller inaudibly.

The hair rose on the heads of the three full-grown men and they drew back from the hole in the floor out of which issued a wailing moan.

The two men flung Silas from them onto the floor and withdrew toward the door backing all the way as if they didn't dare turn their backs on the ghostlike lament from down in the chamber. And as soon as they came out under the shed they broke into a run.

Silas lay still a moment taking stock of his situation. He ought to hurry away, he knew that; he ought to get up and hurry off before the men returned.

"It was their conscience," said the knife-grinder suddenly.

Silas had almost forgotten her; she had been so silent and it was rather hard to see her.

"What?" he said, not quite with her.

"It was their bad conscience," she repeated.

"Oh," said Silas, thinking that he usually couldn't hear other people's bad consciences. He tried to get up but it was as if his legs did not want to obey after having come so close to being killed three times in succession.

"What do you think it was?" he asked quietly.

"It's not the first time they have milled people," she said. "It was the ghosts."

Silas was doubtful.

122

Down in the chamber the ghost began to hum one of the melodies to which Silas used to perform. And shortly after Jef was lowered in through one of the empty windows. Crunching glass beneath his feet, he came over and stood by Silas.

"I'm to cut you loose," said the little fellow.

Silas rolled over on his other side so that his knife could be reached.

"How in the world did you get here?" he asked.

"Oh—that's a long story," laughed Ben-Godik, dangling his bad leg in over the sill to follow Jef.

"We sailed," said Jef enthusiastically.

"In what?" Silas wanted to know.

"Well, first it was something we invented," said Ben-Godik. "We wanted to ferry ourselves across the river on some tied-up bundles of fence posts, but then the current carried us downstream and that's how we discovered that we could sail just as well."

"But did you know where you were heading?"

Silas sat up and rubbed his wrists and still couldn't get over his surprise that the others had got there so fast.

"Not at first," explained Ben-Godik. "We just floated and suddenly ended up out in a long, deep lake —we were lying down on the raft for fear of falling in the water and we stayed lying down right until we beached at the opposite end, where there was a boat."

"Yes," said Silas quickly.

"And where there were a terrible lot of hoof marks of a creature we know very well indeed."

"I was nearly burned to death," said Silas quietly.

"We could see that, but since there weren't any bones in the pile of ashes and we could see the tracks leading on, we thought we must be heading in the right direction—so we took the boat."

"That boat?"

"The other was too dangerous."

"But how did you happen to stop here?"

"I think you hung with your head down just a bit too long today," laughed Ben-Godik. "First, because you put Shags out by the river, and if you think anyone can sneak past him, you're mistaken, and second, we couldn't stop; we crashed right into the sluice gate—and then we obviously couldn't help hearing that something unusual was happening."

Ben-Godik sat himself down as if casually on the pile of sacks on top of the Horse Crone. And though until now she had lain there quietly and unobtrusively just listening, now she let out a bellow that made old flour and sand jump up from the floorboards.

"Isn't it about time you moved the sacks?" she blared. "Do you want me to lie here till doomsday?"

"Yes," said Silas swiftly, stopping Jef, who was already obeying as he was used to doing.

"Leave her right there."

The Horse Crone let loose with her tongue and Ben-Godik turned questioningly to Silas. "Why?" he asked. "What has she done?"

"She killed me."

"I did not," the Horse Crone snarled.

"No?" replied Silas. "Wasn't it you who wanted to get me stuck in the gears up there, if you only could have? Can you deny that? And wasn't it you who told the others that I was there, so that I was also nearly drowned?"

Jef instantly let go of the sack he had tried to move, and the Horse Crone puked over the floor like a hot-tempered dragon. Ben-Godik silently moved a little away from her.

"What did you do with the mare?" Silas wanted to know.

The knife-grinder mentioned a place far back along the path that she had come on, but Silas knew right off that she was lying because the tracks had led almost all the way up to the mill and had only disappeared on the hard-surfaced road out front.

"Free me," ordered the knife-grinder.

"Not before I have the horse!" exclaimed Silas, preparing to leave.

The knife-grinder bit her lips with her long, yellow teeth. Her hat had come off in the rough handling she had received from the miller and his men; it lay by itself some distance away. She looked more ridiculous than really dangerous.

"Jonah!" she bellowed. "I'll break your neck if you don't move this rubbish."

Jef looked in confusion from the woman on the floor to Silas. He didn't know what to do.

"You'll regret it," she hissed when he didn't move.

"How?" asked Silas calmly. "We're leaving now and if the miller comes back, then you'll really and truly lie here. . . . You'll lie here until you rot."

It sounded as if he really meant it, and the knife-grinder howled.

"No, wait! Wait! Your damn critter is a short way

125

down the river—if you follow the road. I swear it—Now let me up."

"Not until I have fetched the mare," insisted Silas.

"Then hurry, damn it!" she roared. "I don't want to be ground to mincemeat."

"Oh," said Silas, enjoying himself. "You know that's an excellent waterwheel. You would be immensely interested to see it from down in there."

"Get going after your horse!" shouted the knife-grinder nervously.

"More silver than you could carry is lying down there at the bottom," said Silas, dashing off. He just managed to see the greedy glint in the knife-grinder's one visible eye before he was gone. Seconds later he came galloping back.

"Now free the lady!" he shouted in through the door.

Jef and Ben-Godik haulted the sacks off her but to their great surprise, she didn't stand up at all; she promptly crawled right over to the hatch and looked down into the empty wheel chamber.

"What did you do with the boat?" she asked.

"In the overflow ditch," replied Ben-Godik. "You can't see it from in here."

Silas led his horse in under the shed roof. He smiled wryly when he saw the knife-grinder on her knees with her nose down in the hole and her bottom up in the air.

"Way back in the corner!" he explained, shouting in to her. "There are iron rungs leading down."

The knife-grinder stretched one hand out behind her, found her hat, and put it on as if she saw more clearly with it on her head. Then she started her descent.

Silas shivered in the wind, his burned clothes, all full of holes, were not of much use.

"How did you actually make that ghost voice?" he asked Ben-Godik, as he looked over the different milling uniforms in the shed. One of the jackets had been patched so many times that it was almost double, and that one he put on.

"There was a crack up by the sluice gate, so I put my mouth to it."

"What about the water?"

"It was above the water—what an echo it made!"

The knife-grinder's broad black hat hung over the hatch eavesdropping for a second, then she vanished into the depths.

TEN

The bear

SOMEWHERE OR OTHER they heard that there was to be a market in the town by the sea. It was the largest town in that whole part of the country and this would be a big, popular market, without a doubt. Even though they already happened to be quite far inland, Silas immediately decided that they should turn around and ride back.

Ben-Godik objected. He said that he would rather go home.

"What about the big summer market?" objected Silas. "It'll be a huge festival and there's money to be made. Lots of money. People pay well when they get in the mood."

Ben-Godik sat down on the ground and said nothing.

He felt that so many different things had happened to them already that he would rather go home.

"You can have half of what we earn," Silas tempted him. "Don't you think your mother would be happy if you brought a little home with you?"

Ben-Godik hesitated.

"A couple of days more or less doesn't matter," said Silas. "After all, you've been away now for almost a year. Besides, Jef lives way out on the coast and we really should deliver him home first—or did you intend to take him home with you to your mother?"

So he gave in.

Although Ben-Godik really did want to return to his own village he could see that what Silas suggested made perfect sense—besides, it was by no means certain that his mother would be particularly enthusiastic about having the family suddenly enlarged by a strange boy. The house was already full and every day food had to be found for them all. Anyway, Jef wanted to go home to his own mother.

When they got back to the town which they had left so hastily that fateful night last spring, they found it very changed. Summer had come; everything looked greener and milder and preparations for the market were already in full swing. On a large flat stretch of meadow outside the town limits, tents had been put up, big tents with small ones among them; covered wagons had been parked and wooden scaffoldings made of thick boards had been nailed together and covered over with sailcloth for stalls and booths along what were to be streets. A crowd was milling about, along with such shouting and bellowing and whinnying that people almost couldn't talk together.

The boys rode in through the outer streets looking around for lodgings, but everything was taken; people from the surrounding region had long since reserved everything—and they had no desire to try the deaf woman's house again.

"What about the farmer where we got the straw?" asked Silas. "He lived out on the other side of the marketplace and he did say that we were welcome to come again."

Ben-Godik liked the idea, and the farmer in turn was delighted to see them, so everything worked out. They immediately moved up into his freshly harvested hay in the loft, and the horses could even have proper stalls because his own workhorses went into an enclosure behind the farmyard. Silas was particularly happy about the horses, because he did not really like having the mare out in plain sight day after day when so many more or less honest people were wandering about the neighborhood. One of the weaker souls could easily be tempted to sell her as his own.

When the animals had been properly installed the boys went down to the meadow to look at everything and join the crowd. The market was to last for two whole days, and even now, the evening before, almost all the booths were up. The place was swarming with half-presentable and decrepit horses and thin cows that had better be sold profitably. There were bull calves and heifers, there were open crates with bleating sheep and wherever there was even one blade of grass left, a goat was tethered. Different kinds of feed, cages, and coops with hens or geese, and big chests with goods to sell stood all around waiting to be put in place.

And more people were steadily arriving.

Lugging big bundles of woolen goods on their backs or pulling even more animals behind them. . . . Walking or driving, carrying everything under the sun. . . . A cart chock-full of easily shattered clay pots came jolting over the grass with protective straw sticking out between the various layers, patiently steadied by the whole family that had made them. Everything that a person could find use for in the course of a whole lifetime could be bought at this market.

The boys wandered silently up and down the streets between the numerous tents looking at everything. Not only tradespeople streamed together but also performers, swindlers, and people with skills like Silas' came traveling.

In one place was a man with powerful muscles who maintained that he could rip horseshoes out with his bare fingers. Even now in the evening he was walking around barechested, showing off.

In another place an ancient, palsied woman sat on a stool by a tent opening. Hunched, with hairy warts all over her sagging face, she was herself a rare spectacle, and her wrinkled neck was strongly emphasized by a pair of excessively bright earrings dangling from her earlobes. Jef stared at her timidly for a long time as the memory of the Horse Crone came alive to him, but in another way. This old woman's fingers were not capable of clamping his arm so hard that he would keep silent; her power was somewhere else, perhaps in her earlobes, which had been pulled way down like leather straps from bearing the weight of the heavy earrings over the years. When he heard that she could read coffee grounds and predict the future for the person who had drunk from the cup, he did not doubt it. It sounded likely. He crept past her small swift eyes at a safe distance and hurried on with a peculiar tingling in his heels.

At other places people were playing barrel organs and dogs with huge ruffs were dancing to the music and in gigantically big tents men played cards and drank ale by lanterns on the plain plank tables.

There were shoemakers who hung wooden clogs up on outstretched lines and a tinker with cooking utensils in clattering bundles, and a place where a woman sat quite still behind a whole mountain of embroidered bonnets and aprons, which she had given up putting into any kind of order before she even started.

Silas sauntered around with both hands in his pockets. He felt at home and at ease in the complex and milling bustle, but both Jef and Ben-Godik went around with big eyes and gaping mouths. Neither of them had ever seen so much of every conceivable thing all in one place, and Ben-Godik was reminded of the peddler with the two chests who had visited his village the year before: He would not have looked like much here. There would certainly be a great deal to tell when he got home, and it was almost impossible to imagine how it could all be even more splendid and multitudinous the next day, when the market was to open officially and the selling to get under way.

But the next day really did turn out as Silas had predicted. All night long people continued to stream in. Behind the tents were masses of wood fires and coal braziers where people prepared the food they had brought with them. A heavy aroma of fried pork and fish wafted over the whole meadow.

With some difficulty Silas found a place for himself and the horse. Since he had no kind of booth to set up, he could not indicate that the place was his, so he found a space on the very outskirts of the market. And very early the next day he began to give performances. Standing on the mare's back wearing only trousers and playing the flute, he let her dance in a circle until he had gathered enough spectators, and then he set to work performing his hazardous capers. And he really carried them off. Even the grown men rubbed their eyes at the sight and the women gasped and clutched their throats in fear-tinged delight. Silas braced himself and jumped like a steel spring and he seemed never to have been in such good form before.

After each performance when the black mare walked around the circle holding the little wooden bowl with the handle between her teeth, offering it to everyone, enthusiasm knew no bounds. Time and again Silas had to change the coins he earned into larger denominations because the money pouch grew too heavy to carry.

Meanwhile Jef and Ben-Godik loafed around the tents looking at what was on display. Silas had given them money for food and a little for themselves and with their hands closed tightly around the coins in their pockets they were content to let themselves be carried along by the stream of people. Neither of them paid much attention to where they were going.

Eventually they came out at the opposite end of the marketplace where a great deal was apparently going on since so many people were headed that way. There they found themselves suddenly face to face with a bear. The bear trainer stood beside it cracking his whip and using shouts to make the bear rise up and walk around on its hind legs.

It was a fairly large bear and when it stood up it seemed even larger. It did what the trainer ordered it to do, but otherwise appeared completely indifferent to him and to everyone staring at it. As soon as the man stopped shouting and cracking the whip, it lay down and closed its eyes, covering its snout with one paw. Only occasionally, when the wind brought the sound of the barrel organs over the general din, did it raise its head with a sign of something resembling interest.

Jef and Ben-Godik watched the bear for a long time, so long that in the end they had spent all the money in their pockets and much later, when they got back to Silas and told him about the bear, he nodded knowingly. Wasn't it just as he had said—that it would be a good market? He wanted to go see the bear himself, but that had to wait until evening; he didn't dare lose his place so early in the day, when it was bound to be occupied by someone else immediately.

In the course of that first marketday numerous transactions were concluded and all were washed down with strong ale in the tents, where there was a rapid turnover of customers. By the afternoon there were already men lying about as if lifeless in the most remarkable places, while a large number staggered and reeled around, yelling and cursing, back and forth between the tents. Then for a while it was as if the hubbub in the whole marketplace abated. After the day's commotion when something was always happening, it was as if lethargy had fallen upon people. They rested awhile, recuperating for the evening when they would commune by lantern light.

Silas stood on the mare's back playing his flute; he too considered taking a longer break and resting awhile. It had been a hard day. Suddenly he heard a terrible scream from across the market, a wild outcry of many voices that went on and on, steadily coming closer. But even though he was standing so high up, it was impossible for him to see what was the matter. It had to be something very unusual; the mare became tense beneath him; her skin twitched nervously and she flicked her ears in alarm.

To keep her calm so that he could remain standing on his high post, he went on performing, and now he played music only for the mare, long, soothing notes calling only to her, sounds not at all like the rousing music he used for his acts. All the while the screams came nearer, and not just a small number of people were involved. Like a wall, a great press of people came tumbling forward along the tent street, a mass of terror-stricken people, knocking each other down to get ahead, overturning everything in their wake, booths and tents alike, wooden shoes and barrels of salted herring. Everything crashed down and broke to pieces under the running feet.

The mare began to shake and tremble under Silas. He quickly sat down on her and led her as far back from the tent street as he could in the limited area.

The first people dashed past without looking to the right or left, and after them came the whole wave of running, yelling men and women with children mingled with them, who all witlessly fanned out over the adjoining fields, dashing through the green, knee-high grain. Then there was a pause during which a few stragglers ran for their lives.

When Silas turned to look down the tent street he saw the bear lumbering along, toeing in, dragging its chain behind it, paying no attention to the overturned booths or their varied contents spread out all over the ground—which ordinarily might easily include something to tempt a bear.

The black mare kicked out and trembled in a way that Silas had never seen any horse ever tremble before; her eyes rolled in terror and there was foam around her mouth as well as sweat on her flanks. He played slowly and gently to keep her calm.

It must be the smell, he thought, the wild, rank smell of bear, which the mare's forefathers must have smelled elsewhere, but which she herself had surely never encountered before.

Unconcerned, the bear wandered down the tent street. In front of Silas' open place it stopped and stared interestedly at him with its small, round, bright eyes. Out in the fields the people stopped screaming; they stood in small clusters waiting to see what would happen now. The bear had come to a standstill.

Silas did not stop playing but directed his flute a little toward the bear and summoned his sweetest notes. The bear listened. Judging from the shrieking crowd that had just recently dashed past, he might have expected an angry, agitated animal ready to attack anyone in sight. Instead, it stood quite calmly listening to his

136

music as if its intention the whole time had been to seek out these fascinating sounds, which the wind had occasionally borne clear across the market hubbub and which filled its ears with so much pleasure.

Silas quickly realized that this bear was used to this sort of handling. Jef and Ben-Godik had told him how its present trainer used angry shouts and a whip to make it obey. Silas switched to a lilting dance melody, immediately triggering the bear to reveal its past training. It rose up on its hind legs and danced, swaying to the music somewhat clumsily without Silas having to say anything at all. Someone must have rehearsed this with it at one time.

Jef and Ben-Godik, who had hidden among the tents when the wave of people poured past, peeked out cautiously now that they heard the flute still playing as if nothing had happened. They had tried to shout to him to run away, that the bear had got loose, but Silas had been unable to hear in the general hubbub, and they had hung their heads in the gruesome conviction that the bear would tear both horse and rider to pieces in his jaws. Now instead they saw a sight that they would not have imagined in their wildest dreams.

The horse was drenched with sweat and white flecks of foam flew from her mouth because she could not obey her instinct to bolt away. Silas held her with his willpower and the bear danced right in front of the rider as if it were his.

"Go get the trainer!" shouted Silas when he caught sight of the two sheepish heads at the corner of the tent. "Tell him the bear is here."

"We can't," replied Ben-Godik. "He's drunk."

137

"Fetch him anyway."

"He's lying on the ground; he's dead drunk. They can't wake him."

Silas thought this over without letting the bear out of his sight.

"Then come over here and hold the mare so she doesn't bolt," he said.

Ben-Godik reluctantly approached along the side of the tents which surrounded the little open space. Silas let himself slide down to the ground and as soon as the other hand grabbed hold of the mare, he walked over to the bear, who looked even bigger from down on the ground.

"They have sent word for the town guard," Ben-Godik informed him.

Silas did not reply. The animal had done nothing; it was the crowd's panic that had given the impression that something wild and dangerous was going on, when in reality the bear was both peaceful and harmless. There was no reason to let it be shot.

But whom could he make understand that? And who could lead it back and tie it up while the trainer lay unconscious from drink? Silas did not need to dwell very long over the answer. Only one person could and that was himself; it was up to him whether the bear would live. Either he would lead it back to its place or else the guard would shoot it.

Playing his flute, he walked back toward the deserted tent street, quietly and calmly the bear lumbered after him, dragging his clanking chain over trod-upon cheeses and dead chickens. It was obviously more used to people

138

than they were used to it, and very probably it had never known a life in the wild.

Silas turned. The bear had stopped by a basketful of eggs that had toppled down from a plank counter and were now slopped out in the sun. The whole front side of the booth had been bashed in against the back wall, presenting a sorry sight. Next to it was an overturned cart of cheeses. The tent street had acquired noticeably greater width on both sides.

Soon after, the bear stopped again. This time the worn-down grass was covered with a select mixture of crushed vegetables and trodden berries, to which Silas let the bear help itself. No one would have dreamed of gathering up the destroyed foodstuffs to try to sell them again, least of all the two little old people who stood completely immobile holding each other's hands in the midst of the mess of ripped sailcloth and broken scaffolding. A wide area of the tent street was covered with what had been displayed on their shelves a short time before. The bear lowered its snout to the ground and began gobbling it right up.

While it was feasting Silas waited kindly and the two old people clung to each other more and more terror-stricken, surrounded by the collapsed scaffolding.

"Can't you take it away?" they whispered.

"But it's starving," said Silas.

"Then just be good enough to take it somewhere else right now."

"I don't think it will do anything," said Silas, "it just hasn't been given anything like this in a very long time."

When he considered that this had gone on long

enough, he called the bear and played music for it, but the desire for berries was apparently still stronger than the desire for music because it did not stop smacking and munching. So Silas collected a whole lot of different things in a basket and held them right under the animal's nose and then it followed him willingly.

But no sooner had they gone far enough from the two old people for the latter to feel safe than they started showering Silas with curses from behind. And he could not make them understand that, first of all, it was not his bear, and, second, it had not destroyed anything.

The old people just went on jabbering in their flat, braying voices. If everything that they wanted to sell had not been destroyed by the loathsome beast, would it have been standing there eating?

Silas shrugged and went on, but more and more disheveled people appeared from their hiding places and let their resentment out on the bear. They suddenly became much braver now that they saw it patiently following Silas back toward the bear trainer's iron stake.

"Thieving animal!" they shouted. "Monster! Well, anyway now it will soon be killed. The guard has already been sent for."

"Why?" protested Silas.

Well, they certainly didn't want to risk life and limb by having such a wild creature wandering around loose.

"Wouldn't it make more sense for the trainer to suffer for this?" asked Silas. "Wasn't it his responsibility?"

"Yes, but he's drunk. There is no way to explain to him what happened."

"Exactly. That's why it's his fault," said Silas.

They didn't understand. Everyone demanded compensation for the terror they had endured, and everyone now saw how cowardly it had been to put their tails between their legs and run away, so to save their honor they went on maintaining that the animal was dangerous. And dangerous animals should be shot.

Even before Silas could tow the bear the last bit of the way to the trainer's corner, two men from the town guardhouse turned up with long guns and lust to kill in their eyes.

Silas' only weapon was his mouth, which he used to protest most prodigiously while at the same time putting himself between the bear and the two armed men.

The guard gruffly demanded that he shut up and clear out.

Silas did not move. Even at a market surely people could not be shot in the open street.

Behind the two men people gathered expecting to be entertained and diverted by the bear hunt. They also thought that there was bound to be very good meat on such a creature.

Finally Silas saw that the only hope was to try to buy the bear's freedom and while he fished out his money pouch from inside his shirt, he asked the two armed men what they thought a bear was worth.

"The pleasure of picking it off," said one. "It's a long time since we've had anything decent to shoot at."

Behind Silas stood the bear with its snout in the basket of vegetables. Silas fervently hoped that it would stay calm.

"What would it cost for you not to shoot it?" he asked,

141

taking two solid silver coins out of his pouch. He laid them on his open palm and extended them toward the guards, whose eyes bugged wide open.

"Where did you get those?" they wanted to know.

"That has nothing to do with it," said Silas curtly.

"Or else they're not genuine—let us test them."

"Go ahead, bite them," said Silas, giving one to each guard.

The two guards stuck the coins into their bearded mouths and swore. Then they asked, "Do you have many of these?"

"Not for you."

The two men hesitated and murmured together; they couldn't very well let themselves be bribed here before the eyes of the townfolk.

"Are you sure they are yours?" they asked, full of suspicion.

"I certainly am," came from Silas.

"How did you earn them?"

"Isn't that beside the point?"

"By doing tricks on the horse," someone shouted.

Jef, who was standing a little to one side, saw that it was a tall man in a leather cap who had spoken.

"What horse?"

A sea of hands pointed back down the devastated tent street to where Ben-Godik stood waiting with the black mare.

"Whose horse is that?"

"Mine."

"That sounds strange. A fellow your age, looking as you do"—here he stared Silas up and down—"with pockets full of big silver coins—and a horse like that."

"All the same, it is true," said Silas, leaning over for the bear's chain and dragging it the last bit of the way to the iron post where he tied it up.

"Perhaps we ought to investigate this further," said one of the guards. "Run over and grab hold of the horse and I'll look after this fellow here."

But before the other seized him, Silas had pulled out his flute and blown a shrill warning signal. And Ben-Godik, who had gradually gathered that something was wrong, leaped up onto the mare and tore off across the fields.

Silas sighed with relief. But to the town guards this was an indication that he had come by the horse unlawfully and from either side they grabbed Silas' arms and started walking off with him.

No one thought any more about the bear. The town guards were sure that they had made a tremendous catch and, all things considered, they could relieve this fellow of his money pouch more easily once they had him in a room to themselves.

And just as if Silas really were an important wrongdoer and solely responsible for the fact that the marketplace looked the way it did, the entire crowd began to follow behind filling the air with curses and insults.

In his cranny between the tents Jef began to weep very quietly, for what would happen to him now? He was suddenly all alone in a milling crowd of strangers, now that Ben-Godik had ridden away on the mare and the two nasty men with rifles had gone off with Silas. He cried more and more as he thought about it, standing there with both hands covering his face, sobbing inconsolably, unaware that a man had come over to his side.

Only when the stranger laid a hand on Jef's arm did Jef give a start. A tall man in a leather cap with a long staff in his hand stood leaning over him, and since Jef could still feel how the knife-grinder used to squeeze his arm if he whimpered, he stopped his weeping instantly for fear that this man would also want to hurt him.

But the man just talked to him in a very ordinary way and said that they had better help each other make everything turn out all right. Jef didn't understand what he meant, but it sounded as if the man was well aware that he had been with the two other boys. In any case he asked where they had been staying, and Jef told him hesitantly about the farm where Shags was still stalled.

The stranger thought that Ben-Godik was sure to return there with the mare when it grew dark.

Jef stared blankly up into his face. How could he know that? But now that the stranger said it, Jef also thought that it sounded likely.

"And when he gets there, you give him this," said the man, rooting around in a leather sack he was carrying by a strap over his shoulder.

Down in the sack were many dark furs and when the man stirred his big hand around down in there it was positively alive with them. Jef stepped back a way, alarmed.

The man pulled various furs half out and then stuffed them back in, until he finally found what he was looking for. With a swift slash he cut the tail off the fur and handed it to Jef, who almost didn't dare touch it.

"Give this to Ben-Godik as soon as he comes and tell him that I'm waiting for him at the bear-trainer's place."

Jef stared down in dismay at the fur tail in his hand

144

but in any case it was not alive. When he raised his head again the man was gone, he could not see him anymore. Still holding the fur piece in his hand, Jef began to run.

Into the town and over to the town hall the two guards propelled Silas before them with their rifle butts. Up the town hall steps, in through the lobby, on through the guardroom and down steep spiral stairs to a massive, iron-plated door. This they unlocked, shoved him inside, and then locked the door behind him. Silas remained standing right inside the door waiting for his eyes to become accustomed to the dim light after the brightness outside.

But before he had even discovered where he actually was, he was greeted by a screeching iron laugh which he had most definitely heard before.

The Horse Crone, it flashed through his mind, the knife-grinder.

She sat straddling a stone bench by one wall with her man's boots sticking out from under her skirts.

145

ELEVEN

Silas
in the dungeon

SILAS LET HIS eyes run around the underground room. Several people were sitting along the other walls, he could see now, scowling, hunched-over men who listened to the Horse Crone's proclamations about the new arrival with obvious mistrust. Her iron voice echoed under the vaulted ceiling.

High up there were holes in the thick walls, broad, V-shaped holes that narrowed toward the outside of the building and ended up as small, solidly barred openings on the square. No one could get out through them, not even a Silas could squeeze through. Nor did they let in much light; down here at the bottom of the dungeon it was dim and bitterly cold. Silas shook himself.

"Ugh, damn it! What a place to stay!" he said out into the gloom, feeling his way forward across the un-

146

even floor, which was covered with broken and fragmented bricks and rubble that other prisoners had occupied themselves by gouging out of the walls over the years. No one had ever bothered to gather up this rubble or even push it aside; it lay where it had been thrown, and so one just had to walk carefully.

Over by the wall sat the knife-grinder, boisterously elated and sharply cutting with her remarks. Quite a while had passed since Silas had last seen her and he wondered how long she might have been sitting there.

"Well now, mill conqueror!" she shouted, moving a little on the wall bench as if to give him a seat. "Show us what you're good for! Make the walls open up!"

Silas did not reply.

"If you can stop the water in the millstream, surely you can also produce a miserable little crack in a quite ordinary dungeon—just as long as we can squeeze through, it will be fine."

"You sound as if you're still drunk," said Silas. "Is the miller's home brew still potent?"

"Shut your trap, pup! I was not drunk, as you well know."

"But isn't that why you're sitting here?" asked Silas innocently. "In any case, you sound as if you haven't quite burned off all that rotgut."

He groped his way past a niche that stank of old urine, revealing that the guard would not let anyone out for such a small matter.

"Do you think anyone could get down those wet iron steps under the mill wheel—and back up again—having tied one on? 'With a bear along,' as we say in the country. Do you think so?"

147

"A bear?" Silas suddenly started to laugh. "Are you quite sure it was a bear that you tied on and not something quite different?"

"Whippersnapper," wheezed the Horse Crone, "you're too young to know what it's like—but just ask them over there if they've ever tied one on."

Silas found an empty space on a bench which had not fallen into too drastic disrepair. He laughed out loud.

"What are you laughing at?" The Horse Crone's tone was sharp and nasty.

"Because I tied one on too," laughed Silas. "I had a bear in tow this afternoon."

"Nonsense," sang out the Horse Crone.

"That's why I'm here now," Silas insisted.

"Empty boasting," came from one of the men by the opposite wall. "You haven't been drinking."

Silas admitted that he had not been drinking.

"But I did tie one on anyway," he said. "And it was so big that the town guards came bearing down on me with their rifles to shoot it."

The man had to smile at the thought, even though he didn't believe Silas one way or the other. But a good joke was not to be scorned in this foul place, and he had nothing against hearing more about the bear.

"Really?" he said. "Then what did you do?"

"I placed myself in front of it so that they couldn't get at it. You see, it wasn't responsible at all for what happened."

"Of course not," replied the man, "you brought that on yourself with your hangover."

"I certainly did not. It was that whole swarm crawling

148

all over each other to be first to get away that did that. They overturned a whole row of carts and booths and everything that was in them. Besides, there was nothing to be frightened of at all."

"What did they think it was?"

"Just a bear."

"Damn it, now you're lying so blatantly I can touch and feel it," laughed the man. "You can't fool me; you wouldn't look so very terrifying even if you did have a jug or two of ale."

Silas was inwardly delighted because everything about the bear could be understood in two ways.

"When does a person get out of this shit hole?" he asked later.

"Not today," one of the men coughed comfortingly, "and certainly not tomorrow either."

"No, because that's Sunday," the Horse Crone interrupted him.

"It certainly is—and you'll be observing it."

Silas glanced at the woman. "Is she going to church?" he asked.

Several men roared with laughter.

"Close to it, anyway. She'll be sitting next to the church door—in the stocks."

Silas pictured the weatherworn stocks outside the church in his mind's eye.

"And the rest of us can't even go up and give her Sunday greetings," the man went on, pretending to be dejected.

"Is that because she stole a child?" Silas wanted to know.

"Oh, did she do that too? No, I think it's because she

won't admit that she's part of a band that steals silver ore from the mine and ships it away. They've questioned her several times. . . . What was she going to do with that child—sell it?"

"No, she just strapped him to her cart with the grindstone and made him pull it."

"How in the world did you ever find one?" the man across the floor asked excitedly.

"I didn't have to look very far," answered the knife-grinder calmly. "All I had to do was pick him up off the beach where he was fooling around."

"Then he was little?"

"Much too little," she conceded. "Not much strength in him."

"On what beach?" asked the man.

The woman let out a cackle.

"Right over there on the other side of the estuary."

Keeping quiet, Silas was all ears.

The man was startled. "Odd," he said. "I haven't heard anything about any child being stolen over there, only about one that drowned. The current took him and they never found him. That was last year."

"Who was that?" asked Silas.

"Oh—I don't recall his name anymore—the father is a fisherman, he often comes to town with his eels and flatfish. My brother knows him."

"Where does your brother live?"

"In one of the alleys down by the river." The man explained more or less where and the Horse Crone screeched scornfully. "So much concern for such a young one. He was really not worth much. Might as well have drowned. Such a weed."

Silas gave no retort now that he knew what he wanted to know. Instead he asked the Horse Crone how far she had got with the miller's silver.

"You yourselves supplied me with a boat," she said.

"Yes," said Silas, speculating how she had towed the skiff through the overflow conduit and out into the stream on the other side of the mill. There had been a lot of stones.

"So you threw the sacks into it?" said Silas.

"Naturally, what else?"

She paused thoughtfully.

Then she said, "But there really should have been oars."

"People always take their oars home with them—that's to make it all the more exciting," Silas suggested.

"—and difficult," added the knife-grinder.

"You expect someone to believe this?" growled one of the hunched men. "That you just picked up the sacks from where they happened to be lying in plain sight?"

"Well, ask him," howled the knife-grinder, pointing to Silas. "He was the one who told me where I could find them."

The men all turned their heads toward Silas.

"Do you know the miller?"

"Only by sight," replied Silas.

"But it seems to me that you're wearing one of his jackets, right?"

"Perhaps you know him?" replied Silas swiftly.

"Not at all," said the man, waving his arms defensively.

"Then how do you know that this jacket is his?"

"Well, I was only asking—we hear so much about that miller these days."

"What do you mean by that?"

"Ask her."

All heads swung back to the Horse Crone.

"I haven't told them more than was true," she said, "and I was sure that he would have done it."

"Chucked us in?" asked Silas.

"Yes," she went on, "down into the wheel chamber and out with the tail water."

The men looked as if they froze.

"But we did get away," said the Horse Crone, scratching herself luxuriously inside her clothes.

"So you're even happy to sit in the stocks tomorrow," came a sour comment from the other bench.

"I'd rather sit there than have two fingers sewn up on the block," came the prompt reply.

"What's that?" asked Silas. "Who gets that?"

"He does, over there."

The knife-grinder pointed to the one who had spoken.

"What for?"

"Stealing, ducky. Fingers too long, so they get chopped off and sewn up. Quite simple."

The man squeezed his hands together between his knees as if he could already feel the ax on his flesh. Nauseated, Silas pulled out his flute so as not to have to hear any more. And, as he had expected, the talk ceased; it was as if the very stones in the thick walls listened. The whole world outside from which they were cut off down there was released in Silas' flute and materialized under his fingers. He played and played and the heavy arched ceiling sang of space and high skies.

152

The men listened quietly to Silas until something rattled one of the small peepholes up on the town square. It was impossible to see anything because it was no longer light outside and in the dungeon it was pitch black. Up by the hole something snorted and grabbed the iron bars so that old mortar rolled down in small brittle fragments. Then there was silence.

"What the devil was that? It sounded like an animal."

"It's my hangover waiting for me," said Silas solemnly.

"Your what?"

"Bear," said Silas. "I tied one on, as you would say."

"But that sounded like an animal—and quite a big animal at that."

"Isn't a bear an animal?"

"Hell, there aren't any more bears around here—that was only in the old days."

"He thinks he's funny," commented the Horse Crone sourly. "Just because he heard a rat—"

"That was not a rat," Silas insisted.

Just then the guard came clattering down the spiral stairs, opened the door, and lit up the interior with his lantern.

"You there with the flute," he called.

"Yes," said Silas.

"Come up here."

"Why?"

"That no-good pest is rattling at the door."

The guard was terrified; there were signs of panic in his voice.

"What pest?" Silas wanted to know.

"The bear, damn it. Hurry up."

153

"Nonsense," said Silas. "It's a rat."

He wondered how the bear had got free again because he was sure that he had done a good job of tethering it to the iron stake.

The guard spluttered.

"Rat!—We almost couldn't get the door closed again; it came halfway in. Now it's standing up there scratching and pounding."

"Oh," said Silas, "does that matter?"

"Shut up and come along; you're to go out and move it."

Silas rose lethargically.

"The others say that there aren't any more bears around here now—only in the old days," he protested.

"If I say it's there, it's there," said the guard. "Come along."

Silas heard the others draw in their breath in astonishment as the door closed behind him and he slowly climbed up the steep stairs.

In the guard's booth the other fellow sat drumming nervously on the table.

"You took your time," he said angrily. And to Silas, "Empty your pockets."

"Why?"

"Let's see what you have."

Silas laid his flute down on the table.

"And your money pouch, too," came the hard words.

"You already got some," replied Silas, making no move to take his money out.

The man at the table made a sign to the other, who immediately grabbed Silas' arm and twisted it around behind his back. With but few motions they had emptied his pockets themselves.

"You're not going to fool us into thinking that you came by this honestly," said the seated man, weighing the pouch in his hand.

The man behind him let go of his arm, but in that same instant Silas sprang upon the seated man and tried to grab his pouch back.

"It's mine," he said. "You can't have it."

The reply was a colossal blow on the back of his neck that sent him right down to the floor.

"That's robbery," snarled Silas, getting up and going over to the wall.

"Exactly," said the town guards, "and you're the thief."

"I'll report you to the bailiff," said Silas hotly.

"I'll give it to you, you runaway bastard!" The guard flew at Silas a second time. "I'll see to it that you're whipped," he hissed while Silas rolled down to the floor again.

Outside, the door was rattled violently once more.

"It's my money," Silas went on. "I want it back."

The other laughed.

"You can come back and get it when you've moved the bear out there—taken it and tied it up properly."

The bear pounded the iron-mounted door with its paws so that it echoed in the hall. Silas saw that this was too much for the two guards.

"Here, take this. Get out there and play for it," the seated man said, handing Silas his flute.

Silas put his hands behind his back.

"I want my money first," he commanded.

"Shut up, go out, and play for it."

"It's not my bear."

The town guards kicked his legs until he was silent, after which one of them twisted his arm again and the other thrust his flute into the pocket of the miller's white work jacket.

"Off you go."

Lopsidedly and hunched-over, Silas staggered across the hall under the weight of the guard's rough grip. The other opened the heavy door slightly.

A black furry snout immediately appeared in the crack.

The two guards stiffened. Then they took courage and all in one motion flung the door open, hurled Silas out, and slammed it shut again.

TWELVE

The stocks
by the
church door

To HIS GREAT surprise Silas did not end up in the arms
of the furious bear but instead collided with a tall man
standing just outside in the dark. The man grabbed hold
of him preventing him from continuing head over heels
down the stone stairs to the town square, and in his
dazed state Silas noticed that this was a very strong man.

On the other side of the door there was complete
silence and Silas could sense the guards listening with
all their might to hear the bear eat him up. The man
took him by the wrist and drew him along down the
steps without a word and, dizzy from somewhat rough
treatment, Silas followed without protest.

"Play the flute," whispered the man when they were
standing down in the square. "Make it sound as if you
were leading the bear away from here."

Silas asked no questions; he heard from the voice that he had to obey, and while he played, they slowly drew away from that dangerous place. Only when they were a safe distance from the town hall did he dare ask where the bear was.

"It's tied up over there," said the man.

They walked over toward the church, while Silas wondered who this man might be.

"But it was over by the door," he said.

"Yes," replied the stranger, "but that was only at first. I led it up the steps and helped it to scratch and pound until the guards came out with the lantern—"

"Yes," whispered Silas breathlessly. He could visualize the men's faces vividly when they opened the door. "And then what?"

"Well, then they closed it again quite quickly. But almost immediately you started to amuse yourself by playing the flute down there in the depths, and naturally the bear wouldn't stand for that. Didn't you hear it over by the hole?"

"Yes," said Silas. "But didn't I see it—over by the door? It stuck its nose in."

The man laughed.

"When it started digging down into the dungeon, I came over and tied it up here, then I rushed over to the door in its place."

"But—"

"You mean—the snout?" The man smiled in the dark.

"Yes," said Silas.

The stranger handed him something and Silas felt the

thing carefully for a long time, whereupon he burst into joyful laughter.

"Hush," the stranger silenced him.

"But it's wood," Silas went on in delight. "Just a piece of wood with hide on it." Then suddenly turning serious, he felt the fur carefully.

"Otter," he said.

The man was enjoying himself quietly.

"Thank you for helping the first time we met," said Silas solemnly, remembering when he sat up in the huge chestnut tree outside Ben-Godik's house.

The bear stood tied to the stocks and beside it stood Jef and Ben-Godik waiting. In the drowsy light from a low-burning streetlamp they looked relieved to see Silas.

"That's where the knife-grinder will sit all day tomorrow," said Silas, pointing to the heavy wood frame to which the bear's chain was securely fastened.

"Who said so?" asked Ben-Godik.

"She did. She's sitting down there in the dungeon waiting. They've put her in the stocks several times since they took her out of the river where she was drifting around in that skiff with all the miller's sacks of silver ore."

"But there weren't any oars," Jef exclaimed, terrified by the thought of that vast river.

"And that made them think that she was on her way to the ocean accidentally against her will—until they discovered the silver, and then they didn't think that anymore. Now they're trying to get her to admit that she was part of the miller's gang of thieves. That's why she'll be sitting out here tomorrow."

159

"But she wasn't," exclaimed Ben-Godik.

The otter hunter went over and began to untie the bear, but Silas stopped him.

"Couldn't we leave it there?" he asked eagerly. "Couldn't it stay there until they bring her here in the morning?"

"Why?" the otter hunter wanted to know.

"They gave me a beating."

"Who?"

"The town guards. They kicked and hit me—and if the bear is sitting here in the morning, they won't be able to put the Horse Crone in the stocks—anyway, not until they move it first."

"And what will you achieve by that?"

"I'll get my money back," came Silas' bitter reply.

"But what if they shoot it?" asked Ben-Godik.

"They can't do that when the whole place is full of people," maintained Silas.

"Will it be?"

"Obviously."

Jef said nothing; he felt sorry for the bear.

The otter hunter chuckled and tied the bear up again.

"But is it going to sit here all alone all night long?" squeaked Jef, his teeth chattering from cold and compassion.

"I'll be here," the otter hunter reassured him.

As a sign that the others could feel free to return to the farmer, he put the leather sack down next to the church wall, swept his cloak tight around him, and sat down on his wares with his legs stretching way out from the wall and his fur cap down over his ears.

So they left.

160

Silas was not really surprised that the otter hunter had turned up. Why shouldn't he sell his hides here, where the big buyers come, the ones who want really first-class fur and who can pay really first-class prices.

It also seemed completely reasonable when Ben-Godik told how Jef had come running with his tongue hanging out and the otter tail squeezed in his hand and had said that the man himself could be found over at the bear trainer's place. It had also been the otter hunter's idea to use the bear to get Silas out of prison.

"But what did the trainer say when you went off with the bear?" Silas asked with curiosity. "Why didn't he bring it himself?"

"Because it looked as if it would be a long time before he could stand up again—if ever. They said that he'd drunk something dangerous—some kind of rotgut, the pig. So he ought to be glad that we looked after the animal for him."

"Yes," said Silas. And they walked on awhile in silence.

"What do you think the guards will do in the morning?" Jef asked carefully a little later. He couldn't stand the thought that they might shoot.

"Make fools of themselves," said Silas bloody-mindedly.

"But what if they shoot anyway? It really isn't the bear's fault."

"They wouldn't dare. What if they hit the mayor?"

"Will he come?"

"Doesn't he usually go to church?"

Jef was silent.

When they got back the next morning, the square

between the church and the town hall was black with people. Like a brush fire, the news of the bear had spread throughout the town, and all who could get about had flocked together to see what would take place. Everyone knew that the Horse Crone would be put in the stocks; the announcement had been posted on the church door for several days—and everyone knew that the bear had overturned half the market the day before. It was almost impossible to push one's way through, there were so many people; Silas and Ben-Godik had to keep Jef between them to make sure not to lose him.

Over by the stocks lay the bear curled up on the cobbles like a big, thick pile of fur; it was quite impossible to see which was its front end and which was its tail; neither tail nor ears could be seen anywhere. It was still sleeping, apparently completely indifferent to the sensation it caused.

But surrounding it there was also a sizable open space, for although everyone really did want to see what would happen, no one cared to get too close. Silas and Ben-Godik could calmly put themselves in front of the circle with Jef and Aaron the otter hunter.

At that moment the door to the town hall was opened and the guards came out onto the steps with the knife-grinder between them, silencing every sound from the gathered crowd. The square waited in an expectant hush, a silence so powerful that one almost could not breathe because of it. It was obvious that the three on the town hall steps were startled and taken aback by the large turnout of people, for not that many usually came out except when someone was to be executed.

With tense and solemn official faces, the two guards

made their way cautiously with the Horse Crone between them, exactly as Silas and Ben-Godik had walked
with Jef. And they went right to the open space around
the bear, almost directly across from the place in the
circle where the boys were standing.

Silas noticed with delight what a start it gave the men
to catch sight of the curled-up mass of fur. They were
seized by a mixture of anger at having been duped and
helplessness in the face of the situation. The knife-
grinder's face also assumed an astonished expression,
but when it really became clear to her what was lying
there, she began to spark and glow like a firewood log
with too much resin in it.

The two gaping guards were not much concerned
with her good cheer and rather gruffly asked her to shut
her mouth, which only made her flaming black eyes
flash with even more malicious glee. And when she
caught sight of Silas facing her, she let out such bottled-
up laughter that her broad-brimmed hat shook on her
bristling wisps of hair.

"Damnation! Who in hell put that revolting monster
there?" the front-most guard exploded. From sheer excitement his voice cracked.

Deep silence.

The guard let his glance run over those who were
standing closest and he stopped accusingly when he
reached Silas.

"It's you, you bastard."

"I am not a bastard," protested Silas.

"You certainly are. Take it away from here."

"I'm not the one who put it there," objected Silas.

"No?—Well, move it anyway."

"I don't dare."

"Why not? Might I ask, weren't you the one who led it to its place in the market yesterday?"

"I have no desire to end up back in the dungeon," said Silas. "I did yesterday."

"If you didn't tie him here, who did?"

The guard stared angrily at Silas, who just shrugged. The knife-grinder shifted her black eyes from one to the other in amusement. Not one of the surrounding bystanders made a sound.

"Answer me!" shouted the guard, grabbing for the rifle as he handed the Horse Crone over to the other guard.

"I did," said the otter hunter calmly.

Something like a breath swept over the square and the whole gathering turned their attention to the tall man.

"Then it's your bear?"

"No," said the otter hunter, "it is not."

"Then why was it put here?"

"Well, it had to be somewhere. We can't just let it wander around loose, can we?"

Meanwhile the bear had become so wide awake that it got up and shook itself, and people drew back a little further now that they could see how enormous it was. Only the knife-grinder didn't seem to suffer from fright at the sight; on the contrary, the longer she looked the more lovingly she gazed at it.

Silas whipped out his flute and played a quick little melody, which promptly caused the bear to rise up on its back legs and start to dance. Afterward it looked

164

around hungrily in the hope of finding something resembling breakfast.

The whole gathering laughed in delight and clapped
their hands, but the guards, who had the responsibility
of getting the Horse Crone properly placed in the stocks
before the church service began, were absolutely enraged. In a nasty, gruff tone they ordered the otter hunter
to move his nuisance and to do so immediately.

"But I told you that it's not mine," he replied.

"Whose is it then?"

The question was fired like a shot aimed at the citizens
beyond him as well.

"The bear trainer's," was heard from several directions.

"Where is he?"

"Out in the marketplace," it was said.

"Then get him. We can't have his wild creature standing here in the center of town."

"It isn't wild," remarked the otter hunter quietly.

The guard obviously thought differently and aimed
his rifle at the otter hunter.

"Fetch the bear trainer," he repeated.

Trouble and alarm mounted in the square. People
stepped all over each other's feet in order to see better;
those furthest back pushed forward while those in front
fought back so as not to come too near the stocks.

"He can't come!" someone shouted.

"He drank too much," said another.

"He'll probably be buried at the town's expense," a
third added.

Something confused and vacillating came over the

guard's face; it sounded to him as if everyone had turned against him.

"You can take him away yourself," suggested the Horse Crone, baring her teeth. "Aren't you supposed to defend the town?"

The guard pretended that he had not heard her taunt.

"Just go over and tie it to the execution block instead," she continued.

"Yes, yes, move it yourself!" others shouted.

The guard whirled around and hit the knife-grinder in the stomach with his rifle butt. But that was a mistake. With a swift motion the huge woman broke away from the man who was holding her arm, and gave the other a powerful shove so that he sat down on his bottom to the great delight of the crowd.

"Then I just might help you with it, dad," she said bitterly, swinging her legs over his before he could gather his wits together. She was over by the bear before anyone could stop her.

"That's right, sister," murmured the otter hunter under his breath as he watched her appreciatively, "just fight back."

Silas looked up at him in astonishment. He had never heard anyone call that huge, strapping person "sister" before, nor had he ever really seriously thought of the knife-grinder as a woman.

Over beside the bear the knife-grinder made little grunting sounds and the particular iron tone of her voice began to sound very strange, but when she started singing a little through her nose, Silas was suddenly aware of what she reminded him of—

Someone playing on a saw blade.

The bear turned toward her, with undoubted interest, and when she changed into the same melody that Silas had played on the flute shortly before, the bear rose up again to its full height and started its dance steps.

Then for the second time it let the bystanders know that it was starving: appealingly it turned its snout toward the Horse Crone and smacked its lips.

And what if the woman didn't start searching in the hidden pockets of her skirts, out of which she drew both a hunk of bread and the butt end of a sausage, which she broke into pieces and offered the animal while people laughed and shouted bravo and jeered at the guard who had cut such a deplorable figure.

The bear sniffed the Horse Crone exploringly and followed her movements with interest when she began to untie its chain. It certainly couldn't have been too thrilling to sit in such a bare, cold place all night, thought Silas, as he and the other spectators moved to one side to clear a path to the block.

The knife-grinder chatted and murmured and smacked her lips and spoke to the bear affectionately and the bear followed her willingly without her having to tug at its chain.

The whole congregation gasped in astonishment.

But the Horse Crone did not stop at the block as she had said and the bear showed no desire to halt right there either. The crowd of people parted in front of them to form an open path; all they had to do was proceed. No one stood in their way or tried to stop the remarkable pair.

Suddenly it dawned on Silas what was really happening and a blissful feeling filled him, for this was much better than he could ever have imagined. Not only had the guards been prevented from putting the woman in the stocks, and for that reason they were the objects of ridicule of their own townspeople, but the Horse Crone had got away. Now she was leaving, simply walking away from both the guards and the stocks and no one could stop her. Silas could plainly see from her back that she was gleeful.

He turned halfway to the otter hunter, but he had vanished, and when Silas looked around for him all his inner joy turned to cold terror.

For the guard had raised his rifle and was aiming right at the Horse Crone and the bear who were moving away side by side.

And Silas was just about to shout out a warning when he saw the otter hunter suddenly appear behind the guard and put one arm around the guard's neck and with the other hand forced the rifle right up into the sky. The shot echoed between the houses, and people flocked together to see what was happening. The path which had stayed open behind the two departing figures closed again, and no one saw what became of them. Everyone had turned toward the otter hunter, who was still holding the guard. Only when the bullet had been fired did he let go of him.

Now the brewing unrest mounted. A whole mass of citizens took the otter hunter's side against the infuriated guards, and Silas pushed his way forward to have a say too. But the otter hunter swept him curtly and clearly to one side, telling him to keep out of it.

"See to it that you get the others out of town as quickly

as possible," he said, "and as far away as you can get. If they catch you one more time, I can't help you. The bear is gone and they'll lock you up because the knife-grinder got away."

"But what about you?"

"I'm used to looking after myself—and they'll take your horse if you don't disappear."

Silas met the guard's hate-filled gaze and no longer had any doubt that the otter hunter was right. Hastily he ducked into the assembled crowd where everyone was shouting at once and, crouching with his head down, found his way back to Ben-Godik and Jef and led them away with him. And while the whole square seethed excitedly behind them, they sought out different round-about ways back to the farm where their horses were.

THIRTEEN

The man whose fingers were bitten

SILAS RODE UP alongside Ben-Godik, who was trotting away briskly on little Shags.

"We'll head straight down to the river first," he said.

"Why?" asked Ben-Godik in surprise. "You said that we had to hurry away, that the otter hunter told us to."

"We certainly have time to deliver Jef first."

The boy in front of him on the mare gave a start at this and Silas was aware that he cringed and seemed to grow smaller.

"But that isn't where he lived," objected Ben-Godik.

"In one of the little alleys down by the river lives a man who knows his father," said Silas. And Jef almost broke his neck craning around to look at him.

"Who told you that?"

"We talked about it in the dungeon."

Silas jerked his head in the direction of the town hall spire, which they could see. They were circling the town.

"About me?" asked Jef.

"Yes."

"Why didn't you say so before?"

"I didn't have time—so many other things happened," said Silas. "I just thought of it now. All this time everyone thought you drowned and that the current swept you away."

"That I'm dead?" whispered Jef. "Mother believes that too?"

"Yes."

"And Father?"

"Yes."

"But I'm not. I'm not drowned, am I?"

"No, but how could they know that?"

"And this wasn't where I lived, was it?"

An anxious, doubting tone entered Jef's voice as if he really didn't know whether he could trust even Silas now.

"It should be over on the other side of the estuary a good way down the coast, they told me," said Silas.

"That fits perfectly," exclaimed Ben-Godik eagerly. "So it was the river that you crossed that first morning."

Jef looked at the river and was silent.

By following the bank they came to the narrow alleys where the poorest people had property. The boys rode slowly, but still the inhabitants glared at them and only answered reluctantly when they asked the way. It took time before they found out how to get to the house that Silas had been instructed to go to.

A redheaded woman with a child on one arm came to the door when they knocked. She too stared at the horses suspiciously; they were not at all used to such means of conveyance in this confined and run-down part of town. She was also not particularly enthusiastic about the excitement they stirred up in the other houses, or that the procession had stopped right at her door. On either side people opened doors and windows to follow what happened better. Silas had to bear in mind that there were other people in the town besides all those in the main square at that very moment.

"What is it?" asked the redheaded woman in an unfriendly way, sweeping a couple of toddlers behind her skirts with her free hand.

Silas gave her greetings from the man in the dungeon.

"Don't know him," maintained the woman, her face turning hard.

"He said that he's your husband's brother," Silas explained gently.

"I don't know about that. He made that up," came the sharp, defensive remark from the woman in the door. She clearly didn't want to get involved.

"Oh," said Silas, and he reflected a moment. People from the alley had quietly crept closer and more inquisitive people were coming all the time.

"Do you know anyone whose boy drowned?" Silas tried cautiously again.

"No," said the woman promptly.

"Yes," quavered a little, hunched-over old woman from the neighboring house. "You do know one at least, I know that."

172

"Not around here," the redhead snapped, irritated at the intrusion, "and not recently."

The little old woman smirked knowingly to herself.

"Where was that?" asked Silas.

"Oh, somewhere down the coast." The woman made a vague gesture toward the land across the river. "It was a long time ago."

"When was it?"

"Last spring, I think. But it's nothing to ask questions about so long after the fact."

"Yes it is," said Silas, "because he didn't really drown."

"What's that he's saying?" quavered the old lady, cupping one hand behind her ear. "He didn't drown?"

"He's sitting here," said Silas, pointing to Jef, who was still sitting on the mare.

People crowded around inquisitively and started to ask questions but the redhead in the doorway was just as unresponsive. And when Silas finally asked her bluntly whether she would take Jef into her house until his father could come and fetch him, she weighed the suggestion briefly. Then she said flatly no.

"Why not?" asked Silas astonished.

"Why should I do that? I don't know him, and how can I know whether he will even be fetched—or whether he is really the boy. Besides, there are enough of us already."

Several people standing around cast appraising glances at Jef, who was crouching in front of Silas.

"Will you pay for him?" someone asked.

"If I had something to pay with, I would, willingly,"

sighed Silas, thinking wistfully of the money pouch which the guards had kept.

"Then he can certainly work for it," suggested someone else.

Jef wriggled; the way they stared at him was horrible.

Down by the riverbank a man turned into the alley and came slowly toward them.

"Here comes Eberhard, so you can ask him yourself," someone shouted. All heads turned to look at the man coming, who in response took stock of the gathering with narrowed eyes. And the silence that spread through the gathering, combined with the somewhat sly manner in which he approached, was felt by all those present as an inner tension.

Just before he got all the way there, he stuck both hands in his pockets and assumed an indifferent expression.

"What a troop," he said. "Where are you off to?"

"South," replied Silas.

"Then what do you want here?"

"They insist that we take that young one there into our house," inserted his wife, pointing incriminatingly to Jef.

"Why the devil should we take him?" asked the man angrily.

"That's just what I've been saying," assented the wife.

Silas hurriedly explained all the parts of the story and how they had found their way there. And Eberhard walked over to the mare's side and stared closely at Jef.

"Have you seen him before?" he asked the redhead behind him.

She shook her head sourly.

From behind, Shags stuck out his muzzle toward Eberhard and sniffed eagerly. The man made a terrified jump quite out of proportion to what had happened, and a malicious laugh spread through the crowd.

"Are you frightened of a little nag like that?" someone shouted.

Silas and Ben-Godik glanced at each other surreptitiously.

"Did you think it wanted to kiss you on the back of the neck?" someone else laughed scornfully.

Eberhard glowered at the horse and did not answer. There was something unintentionally comic about the way he avoided it, and to hide this he began instead to fight with the redhead about whether or not it would pay for them to keep the boy.

The woman said no. Under no circumstance would she have any more young ones in the house; she had more than enough of her own. The man, on the contrary, thought that one more wouldn't make much difference since they already had so many—and of course the father would pay when they got hold of him. And pay plenty.

"Or you could take him home," suggested Silas amicably.

"You go ahead and sail him over yourself. I don't want any more to do with it."

"Nonsense," said Eberhard. "Get down on the ground, boy. Let's see how old you are."

He reached up to help Jef but instead, swift as lightning, he grabbed Silas' foot and tried to twist it around, while he bellowed to the other alley-dwellers to come to his aid.

175

"Now I've got you!" he screamed at Silas. "Maybe you thought I didn't know you. This time you won't get away."

Silas leaned down and tried to wrench his hand away. All of Eberhard's fingers on one hand looked as if they had been crushed not very long before.

A shiver shot through Silas at the sight. Now he knew who Eberhard was and he also knew that if the man had the good fortune to drag him down to the ground, he was finished. He threw himself backwards with the horse so that she tensed and kicked out with her hooves while Jef screamed in terror.

Instantaneously everything in the narrow alley was thrown into confusion. Women and children flapped around like hens in a new hen coop and the redhead threw her apron over her mouth, while the few men who were present prepared to come to Eberhard's assistance. Eberhard lunged at the mare with a long-bladed fishing knife in his hand. If it was the only way he could get Silas down on the ground, then he would certainly slaughter the horse under him.

As soon as Ben-Godik realized what was about to happen, his thought was to ride the man down. Just head Shags straight at him. He jerked the reins and kicked the horse's flanks encouragingly. But Shags was not at all prepared to murder; the man smelt of fish and fish was his favorite dish. Instead of walking over Eberhard's body he sniffed him from his neck all the way down his back.

Eberhard let out a howl and turned from the mare's fencing hooves, promptly transferring his murderous intent to the other, smaller horse.

176

He jabbed at it with his knife.

Using all his weight Ben-Godik swung the horse to one side so that instead of plunging the knife deep into the animal's chest, Eberhard only managed to wound it on the side of the neck.

The horse hesitated a second as if to make sure that this person had evil intentions and had caused the pain. Silas could see how its eyes changed expression while the blood streamed down over its coat.

Then it snorted. Not in delight the way it did with the smell of fish in its nostrils, but a hateful snort. And with its eyes fastened on Eberhard, it approached him.

Eberhard stared wildly back at the old jade, as if it were a ghost; he had never heard of a horse behaving like this. He drew back holding his knife up defensively in front of him.

Suddenly he turned to run in through his door.

But the horse was just as fast, it grabbed him in the shoulder so that the knife clattered far down the alley's bumpy paving.

Eberhard screamed.

And the redhead in the doorway screamed.

And a whirlwind of flapping henlike beings dashed every whichway into their own houses. Shags didn't like to bite; he chewed. And when he let go, Eberhard lay unconscious on the street.

"Strange he hadn't got any wiser," murmured Silas.

"This time he nearly got us," replied Ben-Godik, thinking that Eberhard was only one of the four who had attacked them in the deaf lady's yard.

Without saying more they turned the horses and galloped southward along the river.

Suddenly Ben-Godik noticed that Jef was crying. Not out loud so that it could be heard, but he could see the tears were driven into the hair at his temples by the wind.

"What is it?" he asked.

"Nothing," sniffled Jef, trying bravely to look as if nothing was wrong.

"Do you think you can't go home now? Is that it?"

Jef nodded and bit his lip so as not to cry out loud.

"But you will," promised Silas. "We just have to get away from this town first—then we'll swim the river."

"I—I—can't swim," sobbed Jef.

"It doesn't matter; the black will swim with you."

"But what—what if I drown?"

There was grief in his voice as Jef felt the death that had already been attached to his name and person for so long come nearer.

"You certainly won't drown," promised Silas. "You just hold onto her mane."

"What about you two?"

"You'll see."

Later when they found a suitable place that was not too wide where the current was not too strong, Silas and Ben-Godik drove the horses out into the river. The animals were not particularly bothered by that; they were frightened of the eddies, and the boys had to dismount and lead them by the hand as long as they could touch bottom. But as soon as the horses started swimming, they didn't feel the bank behind them anymore and just struggled toward the bank in front of them. Jef sat up on the mare clinging to her mane as he had been told to, while the water gurgled around his legs

178

and the two others, half-swimming, let themselves be drawn alongside. As long as they kept near the surface of the water they were in no danger of being struck by the horses' hooves.

Safe on dry ground, the mare shook herself so that Jef was nearly thrown, but now he laughed. His relief at not being drowned was so great that nothing else mattered much.

Then they rode on again.

Neither Silas nor Ben-Godik had any desire to spend time making a fire to dry their clothes out. The possibility that people from the town might try to chase them would not completely leave their minds, so they contented themselves with taking their clothes off and wringing them out as well as they could before they put them on again.

On the other hand Eberhard himself might easily not want to make much of a fuss about what had happened. He didn't have too clear a conscience and it could be very costly for him indeed if he had to explain his connection with the silver ore that had disappeared from the mine. He was obviously one of those who, under the cover of his regular occupation, had transported the dangerous sacks across the ocean.

When they came out onto the coast again, Jef gradually began to be able to orient himself. Not that he knew exactly where he was or how far they had to go, but he could see that he had been there before.

For a long time he sat in front of Silas tensely while the horses moved across the heavy sand.

"There!" he shouted suddenly, when they came upon a stretch of dunes and could see far down the beach.

179

He pointed with a straight finger to a cluster of houses ahead of them. "There it is!" he cried happily. They rode over near there and Jef pointed to a house.

"Now you get down and make sure that it is the right one," said Silas, holding the mare still on the crest of a sand dune.

Jef slipped down into the dune grass and dashed off. He stumbled once and rolled over in the sand, got to his feet, and dashed. Without stopping he ran straight in the door and into the house so that the bang of the door could be heard all the way back to where the two riders were.

Then a while passed in which nothing happened.

"What do you think is keeping him?" asked Ben-Godik anxiously.

"He's telling what happened," said Silas.

"But what if they don't believe him?"

"Then he just has to explain why he isn't dead after all."

"What if she can't recognize him now?"

"But she can—look."

A woman came out through the open door with Jef, who was pointing and waving for them to come down there.

Silas and Ben-Godik waved back. Then they turned the horses and rode southward.

FOURTEEN

Ben-Godik's village

So THEY WERE finally homeward bound. Ben-Godik
rejoiced and the horses were given their head, dashing
through many villages without stopping, as long as it
was not so late in the day that they had to look around
for shelter. People turned to watch them pass with surprise and anxiety: What had happened? Had war come?
Had a plague broken out? Because of their tremendous
haste, the boys seemed to be messengers between high-
placed, important people. And in the country villages
people murmured together anxiously when they had
gone past.

For their part Silas and Ben-Godik scarcely talked
together during their long ride. The realization that
they had left the otter hunter in the lurch nagged at
them. He had in fact ordered them to hurry out of

town, and they knew that he was not a person to argue with, but it still pained them to think of him in prison—perhaps even in the stocks. Not even he could lay a hand on a town guard without being punished.

Only when they reached Ben-Godik's neighborhood and could see the houses in the village clustered by the road behind the green fields did they slacken their pace and settle for a more thoughtful speed. It was Ben-Godik who slowed down first. One year had passed since he had left his mother's house, and a great deal could have happened since then. The otter hunter had said nothing during their brief time together, being preoccupied with other things, and Ben-Godik had let himself interpret this lack of news as a good sign. Now he was no longer sure. Now he would have to explain that the last time he had seen the otter hunter he was being led away between a whole cluster of town guards.

Silas stole a glance at Ben-Godik when he slowed down. He guessed what was affecting his friend and remained silent. Ben-Godik had a mother and a couple of younger brothers and sisters he felt responsible for—especially since he had left them without warning. Although Silas did not feel attached either to a family or to a particular place, still he really did understand the other's reluctance to come dashing in between the houses with thundering, crashing sounds when he had no idea how things stood there.

And when in addition to that he thought about their headlong departure from the village the year before, how they had to rush suddenly from the place with a crowd of angry farmers at their heels, it was certainly quite in order to behave somewhat inconspicuously until they saw how things stood. Ben-Godik belonged to this place, nothing would happen to him; he was one of their own. But what about himself, Silas, a stranger who had thwarted the sale of the mare last year, thus preventing these poor people from collecting the money with which to pay their taxes? They surely wouldn't have forgotten him.

Silas decided to use the greatest caution both for himself and for his horse. If he caught the scent of any kind of attack he would take off instantly and ride somewhere else.

Side by side, they let the horses proceed at a walking pace over the yellowish-brown gravel road between the houses. It had almost the quality of a funeral procession, thought Silas. And for the second time he experienced arriving at this village at midday when it seemed like a ghost town. There was no one to be seen on the street; no one was clattering about with buckets or tools or even just talking together. The animals were sleeping too. Even the dogs.

The difference between this silent place and the bustling town by the ocean was striking. There, too, people had rested in the middle of the day and yet they had never seen the whole town resting at one time.

The hooves crunched slowly on the gravel but no one came out to see who the visitors were. By the huge chestnut tree outside Ben-Godik mother's house they stopped and tethered the horses. Silas let his stand way out in the street with the reins loosely tied to a branch, while Ben-Godik placed Shags further in down the narrow passage between Joanna's house and her neighbor's. Neither of them troubled to go in and disturb the noonday rest.

Instead they sat down quietly against the wall of the house facing the street and waited for the village to stir again. Silas could not help thinking of how different everything had been that day when he sat up in the tree not knowing whether he would ever get his good horse back again. Ben-Godik's mother had come out of her house with a bucket on her way to the well, and after her had come Bartolin, who had stopped and followed her with his eyes.

What if Bartolin were inside the house right now?

Silas felt a tingling down his spine as he leaned against the sunbaked wall. He dreaded to know what would happen if that were the case.

"Do you think he's still there—I mean with your mother?" Silas asked in a low voice, absentmindedly drawing with a stick in the yellow dust of the road.

"Who?" asked Ben-Godik equally quietly, turning his head.

"The horse trader? Wasn't he living here last year?"

Ben-Godik shook his head. "No," he said abruptly.

"How can you be so sure?"

"Well, because I'm the one who lives here now," said a voice behind them.

It was the otter hunter. He had come to the doorway without their having heard him at all and now he was standing calmly leaning against the doorjamb studying their surprise with a twinkle in his eye. Both boys stared at him with open mouths.

"Where did you come from?" Ben-Godik finally asked.

"From in there," replied the otter hunter, pointing over his shoulder with his thumb.

"Yes, but how did you get back here ahead of us? Weren't you imprisoned?"

"By whom?" asked the otter hunter.

"The guards."

"Oh, those—"

"Didn't they throw you in the dungeon?"

"I ordered them to fetch the bailiff."

"On a Sunday?"

"Naturally they didn't want to do it," acknowledged the otter hunter, "but then I sent word for him myself."

"Did he come?"

Silas stared tensely at the man in the doorway.

"I was to send you his greetings."

"Me?—He sent greetings to me?" Silas almost shouted incredulously. "Why? He doesn't know me."

"He does now. I told him that all alone, single-handed, you led the bear back to the bear trainer's post and tied him up when he had overturned all the tents."

"The bear didn't do that," protested Silas. "The people did that themselves."

"Yes, but the bear was on the loose. Anyway, as a result you were the one who got it back to its place, and you were the one who tried to buy its life—and it was you who ended up in jail as a result. And if I'm not mistaken they also took your money from you; in any case you stood shouting for your money pouch so loudly that it could be heard clear across the square."

185

"Yes," said Silas. "Yes."

"I told all that to the bailiff. Then there was a worse row, because the guards obviously said that it was all your fault and that everything about the money was pure boasting."

Silas' expression became crestfallen. For a brief moment he had hoped that the otter hunter might have got his market earnings back for him, so that he could share them with Ben-Godik as he had promised. After all, it was not only his money that had been stolen. He lowered his head shamefacedly and didn't notice that the otter hunter sneaked his hand into his coat and drew out a coarse canvas bag. The boy's heart leaped when the man dumped the pouch down in the dust of the road.

"But how—you just said—"

Silas carefully picked up the pouch in both hands.

"They had never dreamed that they would ever be forced to empty their pockets right in the middle of the town square with everyone looking on," said the otter hunter.

There was a pause during which the image of the two men emptying everything out of their pockets in front of the bailiff sketched itself clearly in Silas' mind's eye.

Then he asked, "But how did you get here so fast?"

"Drove," said the otter hunter.

Silas and Ben-Godik looked at him questioningly.

"Plenty of people were leaving there," the tall man went on. "I just had to choose the best and fastest to ride with."

The otter hunter sat down by the wall beside them.

"We fooled that female," he giggled.

"Who?" asked Silas, not following him right away.

"The one with the bear—she certainly cheated them —did you know her?"

"The Horse Crone? Oh, yes." Silas launched into a graphic description of how they had come to her house and what had happened after that and how she had stolen Jef to have someone to pull her cart and what had happened in the gristmill by the river.

Inside the house behind them there was a listening silence. But gradually as the narration proceeded, Ben-Godik's little brothers and sisters came slowly to the door opening, and when they heard how Ben-Godik nearly brought Jef home with them as an extra little brother, Joanna also appeared. The otter hunter was terrifically amused by everything he heard; in particular he wanted to hear more about the Horse Crone, for he had never laid eyes on the likes of her before—or smelled, he added, marveling.

Quite unnoticeably, the other houses along the village street had come alive, heads appeared and disappeared again, feet moved swiftly in the dust of the road and the rumor that the black mare had returned sped through the village like an underground excitement. And this village which so shortly before had appeared dead and deserted began to let out its living beings. Dogs appeared from under the bushes and stretched sleepily; hens rose up from the earth shaking off the dust; children poured out of all the cracks and openings with silent feet and big attentive eyes focused on Silas.

The adults gathered around the horse.

Silas got up watchfully. Ready to run. But the otter hunter laid a hand on his arm.

"Nothing will happen," he said.

Silas did not look at him. Last year at this time the tax should have been paid, he said.

"It was paid last year," the otter hunter informed him.

Nevertheless, Silas could not stay sitting calmly; he placed himself right beside the mare, while Ben-Godik's smaller brothers and sisters flung themselves upon their brother who had returned home. Only one remained standing inside the darkness of the house. From over by the horse Silas could see a pair of feet and a bit of skirt.

She stood listening.

Suddenly she slipped outside, not over to Ben-Godik like everyone else; soundless as a shadow she disappeared around the corner of the house to the passage where Shags was standing half-asleep. There she stood by the wall for a long time.

It was Maria.

Silas stiffened. Why was she still there? Thoughts churned about inside him, for her mother had wanted to sell her to the sword-swallower—at his, Silas', suggestion. The thought pierced him with shame, because then he was not one bit better than the Horse Crone. But how did Maria happen to be in this house? If she was not with the sword-swallower, why wasn't she with her parents on the point in the river? Was it the otter hunter—? Could he have taken her himself? Didn't he say something—long ago?

If Maria had thought that no one had noticed her disappear around the corner, she was wrong. Over by the wall Ben-Godik rose quietly and followed her, and Silas could see the girl start when someone suddenly appeared beside her.

"He's standing right over there," said Ben-Godik, as if he knew what Maria wanted.

Silas tried to pretend that he neither saw nor heard a thing, but everything that happened etched itself into his mind. He could remember all too well what it had been like to meet her and how she had looked under the hair that fell over her face, and he had not forgotten how his own eyes had begun to grow in their sockets because he knew that she had none.

And now Ben-Godik was standing there talking with her as if it was completely natural. And Maria didn't rush off howling like a frenzied animal; she answered him. Silas squeezed his hand tight around the black mare's halter without realizing it.

They talked together.

Maria had tried to hear her way over to Shags, and Ben-Godik had known right off what she wanted. Now he took her by the hand and showed her where he had tethered him.

Silas forgot his own anxiety about what might happen to the mare and walked closer to the two others to be part of this remarkable moment.

Maria flung her arms happily around Shags' neck, while he sniffed and recognized her. She stood that way, absolutely still, with her face buried in the horse's coat, while Ben-Godik patted him and thanked her for the loan.

"He's a crazy one," he said, "but that's also what's good about him. He saved us more than once."

189

"From what?" asked Maria.

"Getting beaten up," said Ben-Godik. "Maybe even from being killed."

Maria turned with her mouth open.

"And every time it was because he didn't behave like other horses." Ben-Godik went on and told how they had been attacked in the deaf lady's yard and how Shags had scraped the two men off against the side panels of the gate.

Without being aware of it, Silas drew even closer. He had never thought that Maria could be talked with like this.

Ben-Godik went on to tell her about the man with the ax.

"Shags came into the barn in the middle of the night and walked around tugging the cows' tails," he said.

Maria laughed and giggled.

"I'm sure he wanted to tell us that the knife-grinder had ridden away on the mare," said Ben-Godik, telling her then how the angry farmer had appeared with his enormous ax and had threatened to chop all their fore-heads.

Then Maria didn't laugh anymore. Covering her mouth with her hand, she held her breath in excitement.

But when Ben-Godik came to the place when Shags had got the upper hand and had danced around after the farmer's shiny ax handle, her spirits bubbled up again.

"In the end he ran away," said Ben-Godik. "Only his wooden clogs were left, so Shags had to make do with one of those."

"Did Shags take his wooden shoe?"

Maria doubted him.

"Yes indeed," said Ben-Godik. "The man took his ax away after all."

"Did he bite into it?"

"He ate it."

"Oh, that's not like him. He never ate clogs at home with us."

Silas felt himself tense slightly. Were they going to argue?

"Then give me your hand," ordered Ben-Godik.

Maria held one out hesitantly.

Ben-Godik took something from his pocket and placed it in her palm.

Then he asked, "What is that?"

Maria felt it.

"Nails," she said.

"What kind of nails?"

She felt them again.

"I don't know."

Ben-Godik put something else in her hand.

"Then what is this?"

"A clamp," came the prompt reply.

"Then what do you think the others are?"

"Wooden shoe nails."

"That was all that was left," Ben-Godik assured her.

Maria closed her hand tightly around them and believed him. And Silas walked silently over and sat down by the wall of the house again with a strange feeling that something was quite different from what he had imagined. And Ben-Godik had known it all along.

The Author

CECIL BØDKER was born in Denmark in 1927. She grew up in the country, with five brothers. After high school she became a silversmith apprentice and then worked as a silversmith in Denmark and Sweden. In 1955 she published her first book of poetry, followed by novels, short stories, radio and television plays. *Silas and the Black Mare*, her first children's book, won the Danish Academy Prize for children's literature in 1967. Several more books about Silas and other children's stories brought her many awards, culminating in the 1976 Hans Christian Andersen medal. Cecil Bødker lives on a farm in Jutland with her four daughters, two of whom were adopted in Ethiopia.